# Carolina Connections

*Southern Breeze Series, Book 4*

## Regina Rudd Merrick

Scrivenings
PRESS
Quench your thirst for story.
www.ScriveningsPress.com

# PUBLISHER'S NOTE

*Enjoy two novellas connected to Regina Rudd Merrick's A Southern Breeze series in one convenient volume. Both of these stories were included in multi-author collections: "Pawleys Aisle" (Coastal Promises) and "Mr. Sandman" (Candy Cane Wishes and Saltwater Dreams). Now you can complete your collection of A Southern Breeze stories with this novella duo, Carolina Connections.*

# Pawleys Aisle

*A Novella*

## Regina Rudd Merrick

Scrivenings
PRESS
Quench your thirst for story.
www.ScriveningsPress.com

# CHAPTER ONE

"*O*h, Ms. Bertie, why didn't you tell your grandson what we were about?" I know that raising my eyes to heaven and talking to a lady who's dead and buried won't get me anywhere, but if it makes me feel better, why not try it?

Honestly, the first time I met Marc McCallum, my first instinct was to try to draw him out of his shell. I mean, he's a writer. I get it. He's serious. I get that, too, I suppose. But shouldn't using your imagination for a living be fun? The wedding vendor in me, and comments from his beloved Granny Bert, notes that he is single and seemingly proud of it. If I hadn't embraced singleness after my experience with Daniel Rogers, I might notice his good looks in that smart-guy, slightly-athletic-but-nerdy sort of way, which I usually find attractive…But sworn off men I have, so that's that.

Now what to say? I'm here, at the front door, letter in hand, and I'm speechless. And mad. "Okay, Lord, give me a little calm before I make a fool of myself." As soon as I knock on the door, I hear frantic barking, and then a distinctly masculine voice shout, "Quiet, Muffin!"

I have to snicker. It's one thing to hear an elderly woman

calling her sixty-five pound Golden Retriever "Muffin," but McCallum?

The door opens and Muffin immediately pushes her way around her new master and sits in front of me, waiting for her hug. "Hey, girl! How's it going?"

"Miss Prince." He stands there, all six-foot-lean of him, shoulder hunched on the door frame with his arms crossed, as if I'm a bother he could do without. He looks down at Muffin and frowns a bit. I wonder if he's jealous of the rapport between me and this big hunk of golden sweetness.

Probably.

"Mr. McCallum. Do you have a moment? We need to talk." Rattling the paper in his face is tempting, but I'm trying to use my big-girl manners.

The twitch of his lips shows me he has to think about it. Get over yourself, bro. He seriously looks at his watch as if he's in the middle of peace talks or something. Then he scratches nervously at his beard and comes to himself. "Come in. Would you care for something to drink?"

Surprise, surprise. He has big-boy manners. "Uh, sure. Water or tea is fine."

"Good, because it's all I've got."

This place hasn't been dusted in weeks. Ms. Bertie would be scandalized.

He draws in a breath, bringing me back to the present. "Hot or cold?"

"Water?" I can't resist.

"I meant tea."

Wise-guy. "Cold is fine, if you have it."

He pulled the tea pitcher out of the refrigerator. "Unless you want some milk that expired three weeks ago."

"No thanks."

"I suppose you got the notice."

His tea-pouring skills are decent. At least he keeps the

kitchen sanitary, and Muffin's food and water bowls are sufficiently filled for this time of day. Who am I? A representative of dog-protective services?

"I did. And I thought it was time we had a talk about what your grandmother, Ms. Bertie, and I were up to."

"That's an interesting way to put it. Knowing Granny Bert, there's no telling what she put you up to, and no telling what wild schemes you roped her into."

Cut to the heart. "Now listen here, Ms. Bertie was a sweet, gentle soul who never led anyone astray, and I'd like to think the reason we clicked was that we were a lot alike." Pressure. Right there. In the middle of my chest. And the pesky tears. They only come when I'm frustrated or hurt to the core. Right now I'm not sure which I am more – hurt or frustrated. Muffin pads over to me and leans against my leg. What a good dog. "I know. I miss her, too." Sniff.

Now he looks frightened. Tears often affect men in such a way. You work in the wedding biz, and you know all the signs. A woman even hints at crying, and every male in the vicinity gets glassy-eyed and red in the face. For some reason, this little bit of knowledge helps.

"I'm sorry to mess up your plans, but I'm trying to work here, and if I have people in and out of the garden at all hours, I can't settle down to actually typing the words."

"Don't you think 'at all hours' is overstating it a bit?"

At least he has the grace to look sheepish as he holds his hands up in a defensive move.

"Maybe. The problem is I never know when a spark of inspiration is going to hit. It might hit right in the middle of one of your soirees, and then I get distracted by music and noise, and I'm sunk."

"Is inspiration really that finicky?" Who knew? I was under the impression writers could just sit and type away, a novel springing from their fingertips.

He has a nice laugh, but that is definitely not the point right now.

"Yes, it can be that finicky."

He gestures to the kitchen table and I sit down, jiggling my glass of tea nervously. I seem to have an unreasonable need to make sure my ice cubes do not stick together. Muffin flops down at our feet. Maybe she is playing the role of mediator.

"Mr. McCallum, I don't want to be a nuisance neighbor."

"And I appreciate it."

He's sitting there, looking at me. Now, could I please be a reasonable adult about this?

"When I bought the Chapel, it took every bit of money I had saved, and then some. I borrowed the rest based on my business plan, which your grandmother helped me to develop."

Ah, he looks surprised. His little granny wasn't smart enough to be a financial adviser?

"Granny Bert?" His eyes widen and he seems stunned.

"Do you have another grandmother in the neighborhood?"

"No, my other grandmother lives in Columbia."

"Bless her heart." How can anyone live inland, when there is this entire coast in South Carolina?

His lips curve into a rueful grin..."Tell me about it. Why do you think I'm here instead of there?"

"You grew up inland?" Could explain his grouchy demeanor, singleness notwithstanding.

"I did. Granny Bert's house was home in the summers, though."

"She talked about you a lot." Should I tell him one of her greatest wishes was to meet her great-grandchildren before she died, and that she despaired of him ever producing an heir at the rate he was going? Probably not.

"Did she?" His face softens. "She was something else."

I know I'm frowning, but I can't stop. "I'm confused."

"About what?"

"If Ms. Bertie was so important to you, then why would you accuse her of 'putting me up' to something? She was an angel in disguise, if you ask me."

Something about his face seems to close off suddenly. A little stab of guilt? Funny how in the six months I've lived here I never met him until two weeks ago, after Ms. Bertie's death.

"I'm sorry." I finish my tea and rise to set the glass on the counter. "I didn't come here to discuss your relationship with your grandmother, although I would have thought you would be interested in her business investments."

"Investments? You mean she actually invested in your business?" He slumps in his chair, closes his eyes, and sighs.

"Well, yes. It wasn't much, but she wanted to be a part of getting couples off to a good start. Her investment was letting me use the gardens for receptions and pictures, and other events. She didn't invest money. She invested her time and talents in me."

# CHAPTER TWO

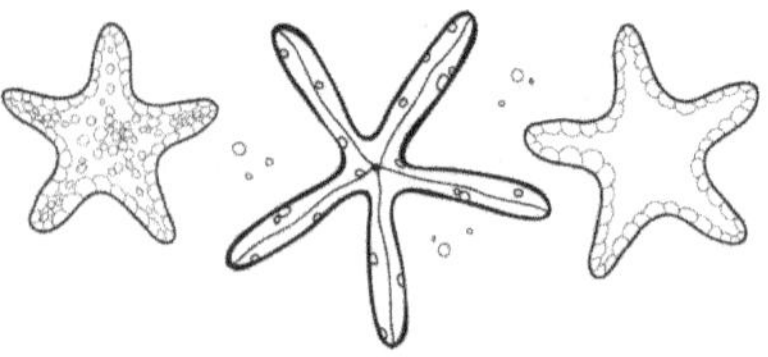

When did I realize I had given up on marriage?

Maybe it was when I bought the old Pawleys Island Chapel and decided to turn it into a wedding venue.

If I can't have a happily-ever-after, I won't begrudge the loving couples of the Pawleys Island area their day of bliss. What can I say? I'm a sucker for love and romance, especially when I'm not involved.

But who knew second-hand bliss was so expensive?

Looking at the spreadsheet on my computer, I know the numbers aren't adding up to a profit. Not yet, anyway. There's still so much to be done. Renovations, which include upgrading the restrooms and putting in a kitchen, and then my salary, which right now is a big fat zero.

Leaving North Carolina and moving back to my parents' house in Myrtle Beach had been hard. They didn't understand why I would give up my position to go into a business that seemed to be sunk before it could get going. Without going into too much detail, I told them I didn't have a choice. I had to leave Charlotte. I'm pretty sure they were afraid to ask at that point.

I've made my decision, and I'll stick to it. Never again will I be at the beck and call of a boss who doesn't care as much about me than about his bottom line. Especially when he claims to love me. I still feel a stab of hurt and fear when I think about the whole situation.

And now Ms. Bertie is gone. She was an oasis of sanity in this crazy new world of adventure of owning a business that depends on goodwill and excellent customer service. Corporate banking was no preparation for this kind of work, but I'm finding it oddly satisfying, putting out little fires here and there instead of negotiating interest rates and terms for the next step in a company's ladder of progress.

Weddings don't just happen. As in banking, there are months of planning, promises to keep, and bending over backwards to provide what the client wants. It can go like clockwork, or it can explode when one piece of the puzzle goes off-kilter.

And there are days when it doesn't take much for a situation to go AWOL, awry, nuclear.

In this instance, off-kilter's name is Marc McCallum, Ms. Bertie's grandson.

Just thinking about him raises my blood pressure and makes me rant inside. Unusual for me. I'm usually calm and collected on the outside – a trait Daniel never seemed to understand and constantly criticized me for – but now I'm a raging inferno who wants to run my business and get along with my neighbors, and who isn't afraid to approach them if they are being unreasonable.

And Marc McCallum is being not only unreasonable, but disagreeable as well. Making terrific sweet tea does not excuse him from the blight overtaking my business and ruining my life.

Maybe ruining is an overstatement, but Ms. Bertie would be appalled to know her own grandson is standing in the way of the business we created over many cups and glasses of tea, mulching sessions, and prayers.

"Chelsea, Hun, would you bring me that spade over here, please? I think this plantin' bed could use another gardenia."

That's how I want to remember Ms. Bertie: Always into something, whether it is in her beloved garden or my business. This was the lady I thought of as my "third grandmother," mentor, and friend. The day I took possession of the chapel, she came across the garden with a tray of sandwiches and brownies, and a pitcher of her extra-sweet tea. We had a picnic on the stoop that entered her side garden. Even covered with dust and cobwebs, she loved me at first glance, and I loved her right back. I heard about her grandson Marc that day, and eventually about how she wanted him to find a woman before she was too old to enjoy her great-grandchildren.

That's why it stung so when Marc's first encounter with me, at the house after the funeral, was him questioning all the dates marked on Ms. Bertie's calendar with my name on it. As if I were trying to bilk her out of something. What, I had no idea. Ms. Bertie never seemed to have any financial troubles, but didn't live high on the hog, either.

My desk is covered with folders of the weddings coming up in the next six weeks. Four of them had booked Ms. Bertie's garden for their small reception, and I either had to find an alternative – which would not be as cost-effective – or cancel them outright, which could be disastrous for my business.

It doesn't help that Jake's and Lydia's wedding is one of them. My brother will never let me hear the end of it if I change his wedding venue now.

Looking out the window of the office, right into Ms. Bertie's garden, I see Marc sitting on the loggia, staring into space. Maybe his creative juices were overwhelming him. He certainly wasn't getting any interruption from me right now.

Scrolling through various venue websites, I pause on Emmaline Quince-Jernigan's website. She has a fairly extensive list of reception venues, including Pilot Oaks, an antebellum mansion owned by the Crawford and Benton families. Rance and Charly's wedding was beautiful, but it was more ornate than many of my clients want. A couple choosing a wedding venue seating a total of eighty on a full day wants something simple and quiet.

This is a hard concept to get into McCallum's head, apparently.

My phone ringing reminds me I had left it on a louder setting than usual after walking on the beach. After a moment of checking the caller ID and calming my erratic heartbeat after the startling sound on my desk, I pick it up.

"Hello?"

"Miss Prince? It's Marc McCallum."

Looking out the window, I can see him, still on his back loggia, his phone to his ear. He sees me in the window and waves as I pull my head back quickly. Drat. It's not as if I'm stalking him. I can't help it if my window conveniently looks out upon Ms. Bertie's beautiful garden I helped to plant.

"What can I do for you, Mr. McCallum?"

"First, you can call me Marc, and second, we need to talk."

"About?" I'm not going to tell him he can call me Chelsea until he bends a little. Sour grapes, much?

"About our...situation."

"Would this have anything to do with a legal document that was served to me? I wouldn't want to break the law or anything." Take THAT.

"Can I come over? I'm willing to meet you on your turf."

My turf, huh? Actually, I don't own any turf. Just sand. He has the turf I need. I make the decision to be grown-up about it. Again.

"You may. I'm not sure what we have left to talk about."

"I have an idea, and it may be to both of our benefits."

"Very well. Come on to the back door and I'll meet you."

Beep. Beep. Beep.

He hangs up. Rude.

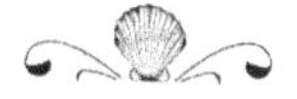

"WHAT IS this grand idea you have?" I indicate a folding chair across from my desk. No comfy chair for this Bozo.

"A compromise."

I lean back in my chair and cross my arms. A classic defense move.

"As in?" My left eyebrow automatically rises. I will let him do the talking. He knows my position, and he knows his withholding Ms. Bertie's garden has thrown a monkey-wrench in my plans.

He leans forward, elbows on his knees, hands clasped between them. He takes a deep breath, releases it, and looks me in the eyes. "I think we can make this work."

I'm afraid to breathe. I know my mouth must be hanging open. Is he capitulating? Is he really going to let me continue using his property as Bertie and I had planned?

He holds up his hands quickly. "At least for the weddings already scheduled, as long as they don't interfere with anything I might have planned."

I start to chime in, and instead clamp my lips between my teeth. Now was not the time to whip out a barbed response. What's the phrase? Oh yes. Don't look a gift-horse in the mouth.

"All right, what are your terms?"

"You get to use the garden and downstairs rooms in exchange for caring for the garden."

My eyebrows stretch to their limits. "That's all?"

"And I have to approve all plans taking place on my property."

"I see." The eyebrows go down. "In other words, if you don't like a theme or a particular type of music the couple wants played, you can veto it?"

"In theory, but probably not." He rubs the back of his neck. "I'm not an ogre."

Coulda fooled me. I hope I didn't say that out loud. I hope my face didn't say it out loud.

"Let's start with this: how many weddings do you have scheduled to use the property?"

"Four, within the next six weeks." I hold the four folders toward him, which he takes and opens. He looks slightly taken-aback. I'll hold out on telling him about the weddings and events scheduled three years in advance.

"You're very thorough."

"Yes, I am."

"Where did you learn to do reports like this?" He looks at me as though he's never seen me before.

"First at Clemson, then at USC Moore Business School." I sit there, waiting for his response.

He stares at me in silence. "You went to Moore, in Columbia?"

"For my MBA."

He sits back in his chair shaking his head, his eyes narrowing for a second. "Let me get this straight. You have an MBA from the top business school in South Carolina, and you let my grandmother help you with your business plan?"

My shoulders lift involuntarily in a shrug. "Yes. I needed someone to help me put more humanity in my business. My former work as a commercial mortgage broker doesn't really lend itself to the touchy-feely business of weddings, now does it?"

And now he's thinking I must be smarter than I look, or I'm an absolute flake who wants to run a crazy wedding business.

"Probably not." He looks down at the report in his hand, flipping through the pages of the binder. "I thought you were just..." He has the grace to look sheepish.

"Just what? A fly-by-night entrepreneur? A woman running a wedding chapel until she can get 'her own man' and settle down to make babies?"

"Now you're putting words in my mouth. Although the first was a fleeting thought."

"Your grandmother and I spent hours discussing what a wedding business should and should not look like. I shared things with your grandmother I've not shared with another soul on this earth." Oh no. I'm standing, hands on hips. When did I stand up? My face is hot, and I can feel tears prickling behind my lashes. I will not cry in front of Marc McCallum. Not for all the tea in China. Get a-hold of yourself, girl. He's trying to make nice, and you're going to mess it up.

He stands and places the folders on the desk, leaning on it, bringing his height down closer to mine. "Chelsea …"

"I didn't say you could call me Chelsea." Now I sound pouty, even to myself.

"Miss Prince, I apologize." He stands there, looking me in the eye, waiting.

After what seemed like eons, I have to break the stare and sniff. Loudly. His lips are still set in a firm line, but they're beginning to crumble into a grin. He breaks eye contact and looks to his right where there is a tissue box, and grabs one, handing it to me.

I blow my nose, trying to use every inch of the tissue, but it isn't enough. He reaches down, reading my thoughts, and hands me another.

Finally, I look up into his green, gold-flecked eyes and force my shoulders into their normal position. "Apology accepted."

"Are you sure?"

"Yes, and you can call me Chelsea."

# CHAPTER THREE

"I'll need ten round tables, and two eight-foot long tables for the head table."

Why do I love going to Hodge's Rentals? It's a smorgasbord of wedding paraphernalia – if you are old-school and want candelabras, they have them. Chuppah for a Jewish wedding? Yep. All kinds. Simple planters with fake ferns? Of course. And chairs? They have chairs by the kazillion, from bohemian floor pads to formal Chippendale dining chairs to tulle-wrapped straw bales for that one-of-a-kind country wedding.

"Did you decide what kind of chairs you want for the reception?" Ken Hodge has his checklist in hand as I tap my finger on my chin, pondering the array of seating options.

"I'm thinking the gold bamboo. What do you think?"

He grinned. "I think they'll be the bomb."

"You're no help. I'll take some pictures and call you with the final word from Jake and Lydia. I should have brought them with me." I snap the images and walk over to the chunky candle holders. These would be perfect for the relaxed vibe Lydia wants. I snap a picture in case I need to send it to Lydia or the wedding planner, Emma.

"This is your little brother's wedding you're talkin' about?"

"Yes, but at six-foot-seven, he's not so little." I chuckle when Ken's eyes round.

"Now that's a tall drink of water. Did he play basketball?"

"Unfortunately for his educational expenses, no. He was too busy playing video games and putting computers together. Now he teaches special education in Georgetown."

"Important work. My sister's girl is in special ed. Diagnosed with dyslexia when she was seven, and she's a teenager now and reads as well as I do."

"That's great. So much can be done now to help kids." Stories like this make me proud of my brother and makes me wonder why I chose such a worldly occupation.

"Yeah. I'm thinking about hiring her to help out over the summer. She's good with people, and it would give her some experience." He shrugs, reddening a little.

I don't know Ken well, and I just learned an important fact about him – he is a teddy bear.

I look up when I hear the door open. An attractive couple enters the building holding hands. The light is glaring, and it's a second before I recognize Emma and Rafe Jernigan.

"Chelsea! So good to see you." Emma tugs her hand away from her husband's and gives me a quick hug. A true Southern Belle, Emmaline Quince-Jernigan is the owner of Quince Wedding Designs, and is partnering with me in creating Lydia and Jake's dream wedding.

"Oh good! You're here for your brother's wedding, aren't you?" She smiles and glances over at Rafe. "You know Chelsea, don't you?"

He holds out his hand, a smile on his rugged, freckled face. "I think we met at Charly and Rance's wedding, didn't we?"

"Yes, I'd recently moved down about then, and Charly insisted I come. It was a great way to meet folks."

And a great way to figure out what my next calling would be.

I tagged along with Charly and Lydia at the tail-end of her wedding preparations, and between that, meeting Emma, and finding the chapel on its last legs, my fate was sealed.

"Well, Chelsea, I'm glad you're here. I know you're getting the tables and chairs, and I've been commissioned to get the flowers and tablecloths for the tablescapes. I wonder if there are any other things I need..."She looks around, tapping her chin with a well-manicured nail.

"Oh! Did you see the chunky candlesticks? What do you think?"

Emma walks over to them, then looks up and smiles. "These are new, aren't they, Ken?"

The owner grinned. "Yep. I had a feeling you'd like those. When Chelsea saw them she was as happy as a flea in a dog house."

Emma laughs, then places her finger on her chin, thinking. "I love them. Do you think we could use them somewhere? They would be beautiful in the garden set-up."

I felt a muscle in my eyebrow begin to twitch.

"What's wrong? Don't tell me that man has changed his mind again?"

"Marc? No, I'm trying to avoid him whenever possible."

Emma shoots a glance at her husband and twists her lips ever-so-slightly before turning back to me. "And why would you want to do that?"

"He irritates me. That's all."

"Oh?"

Please, tell me my face isn't getting red, because suddenly this normally ice-cold showroom is getting a little warm and claustrophobic. Marc does irritate me. I haven't quite worked out why, at this point. In the meantime, I'll keep some distance between us. Hmmm...Maybe I'll try a little match-making and find him a wife. Maybe then his irritation-index will go down a little.

# CHAPTER FOUR

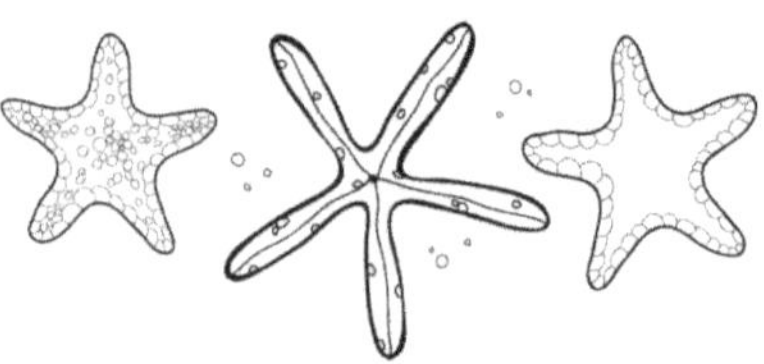

Four weeks until Jake's wedding, and only one week until the Stafford/Brundage wedding. The upcoming wedding features a restaurant reception, so Marc won't be bothered. Should I really be sitting on top of this ladder? Probably not. Seeing the frown on Marc's face as he sits in front of his laptop on the loggia, I hope I'm not distracting his "muse" by stepping onto his property to maintain my own building.

Trying to ignore the gentleman across the yard, I'm determined to focus on positive thoughts. If he can ignore me, I can, in no uncertain terms, ignore him.

Wireless ear-buds firmly in place, I turn up the praise music on my music app. No, I will not listen to Mandisa's "Good Morning." I have my limits this early in the day. Tap to skip to the next song. "Good, Good Father."

Ah. Much better. And I do have a good, good father, both earthly and heavenly. It's true that my earthly father, whom I adore, doesn't understand why I decided to leave the lucrative field of banking for what sometimes seems like the thankless job of wedding-venue entrepreneur.

If he knew what happened with Daniel, he would be traumatized, as I was. The idea that someone I trusted would undermine my confidence to the point I could almost let him...I won't go there. It's a new day, and God made a way for me to be in the sunshine, to help couples get a good start at a good price. And He has blessed me beyond measure, if you don't look at the bottom line.

I could feel the smile lifting my cheeks. If anyone should know a business takes time to get off the ground, it is I. There were new businesses, back in my banking days, which hung on my every word when it came to their success or failure. And here I am, worrying, when God flat-out told us not to worry about anything, but to pray about everything. Duh.

Then why do I have a nagging heaviness in my chest when I see my bottom line getting smaller and smaller? Maybe I can't do this. Maybe I'm not smart enough to make my own way. Book-smart, definitely. Business-savvy? I'm not sure.

Focus, Chels. You've got this. God's got this.

I glance over and notice Marc leaning back in the wrought-iron patio chair, hands linked behind his head as he stares off into space. Must be nice to have the life of a writer. I mean, don't you simply sit and wait for the stories to fill your mind, then you type them out?

There is one spot on the window frame that I can't... quite...reach.

The ladder seems a bit shaky, which does not help my queasiness at being up this high. Maybe I should shift this way a little...wait, is that me screaming? And falling? And what are all those black dots...?

# CHAPTER FIVE

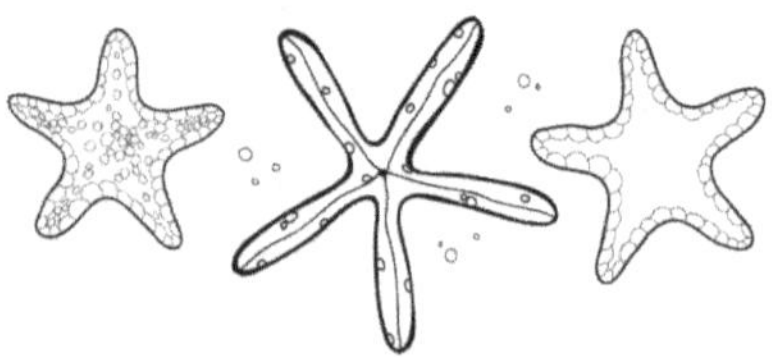

hen I open my eyes, I realize I'm laying flat on my back, and there is a pair of brilliant green eyes staring down at me. They are rather nice eyes, even if they belong to Marc.

"Are you okay?" He's kneeling next to me as if he's unsure what to do. "Do I need to call an ambulance? Can you move?"

I blink my eyes and turn my head, noticing that there seems to be one spot that hurts, and my chest is burning as if I've run five miles. Am I having a heart attack?

No, a memory comes flooding back of first grade and getting left on the upper level on the see-saw. My friend – whom I never felt the same about afterward – jumped off the see-saw as soon as the bell rang to go inside, leaving my half of the see-saw – the "up" half – to plummet to the ground so fast all the breath whooshed out of my lungs leaving behind tears and incredible pain.

When I lift my hand up to touch what feels like a softball protruding on the back of my head, my eyes widened. "I think so?" I move my feet to sit up and turn my head again. "Ouch."

"You had quite a fall. Here. Let me help you." Marc put his

hand on my elbow to steady me and I feel a sudden urge to let him help me all the way to my feet. Not that I'm attracted to him or anything. That would be weird.

When I get to my feet, he continues holding onto my arm. "Thanks. What in the world happened?"

He points to the bright yellow label on the eight-foot ladder, now lying on its side. "Ladders have these nifty warnings on them not to sit or stand on the top."

That was unnecessary. Well, maybe not. But still. Kick a girl while she's down?

"I am aware." I point to the window where I had been working. "I couldn't get to the top part of the window to replace the glazing." Sigh.

He shakes his head and gives me a twisted grin. "You don't have to do everything, you know."

"Somebody has to, and since this is my property, I've committed myself to doing as much as I possibly can without paying someone to do it." Because every cent that comes in from a client goes right back into the place. Eventually, I'll be able to host things on a grander scale. For now? I'm glad "rustic" and "shabby" are still in fashion.

My ire was giving me a headache. Or maybe it's the whopper on the back of my head. I touch it tenderly and wince. No blood, at least.

"Here, let me take a look." He gently parts my hair and probes with his fingers. "You've got quite a bump there, but the skin isn't broken. How do you feel?"

Feel? I feel a glare coming on, and it has nothing to do with him and everything to do with being embarrassed. "Dumb and stupid and like I can't do anything right."

He laughs out loud. I should be irritated, but instead, I'm amazed. He has a great laugh. I've never heard it before. Not like that, anyway. In my mind it has always had a mean-spirited edge to it. Maybe I've been biased.

He grins and raises an eyebrow. "That's a little extreme, don't you think? I meant physically."

"I'll be fine." I sit down on the stoop leading from my chapel to Marc's yard and straighten my back to take in a deep, painful breath before I slump in despair. "It hurts, but I'm fine." I lower my face into my hands. "Sometimes I wonder why I try."

He sits next to me on the step, not touching, but close enough if he wanted to. "I know what you mean."

"Come on, best-selling author, inheritor of this fine estate?"

He looks across the yard at his grandmother's house, now his. "Bestselling is a stretch, although some of my ghost-writing has done pretty well."

"You write for other people?" I tilt my head and look at him in surprise, which hurt. "Ouch. Remind me not to do that."

"Somebody needs to help you keep your head on straight." His grin had me tilting my head again.

"Cute." I sit there, willing my head to stop pounding. "Ms. Bertie said you are an associate professor at USC Columbia. How do you write novels and teach, too?"

"It isn't easy. I do take my summers, which gives me some uninterrupted time. When were you at Clemson? I don't know how I could have missed you."

I feel a little hiccup in my system, and tamp it down. He's not my type, remember? Besides, I'm going to continue Ms. Bertie's work and find this man a woman to marry. It shouldn't be so difficult. He looks nice, even if he has a mean streak when it comes to neighbor-entrepreneurs. I clear my throat and down-play any hidden meanings. Probably so hidden HE doesn't even notice it. "Big school, and I graduated early, in December 2008."

He nods. "That explains it. I earned my doctorate in 2005 and started teaching at USC Columbia right after. "

Shocker. He's more than five years older than me?

"You seem surprised?"

"I didn't think you were that much older than me."

He shrugs and looks away. "I crammed a master's and doctorate into three years. Sometimes I wish I'd taken a little more time and spent more time down here."

"She missed you."

"I know. I missed her, too." He looks over at me and gives me a half-grin that tells me he's a little sad. "Life, you know."

"Yeah. I know." I wrinkled my nose. "Sometimes life stinks."

# CHAPTER SIX

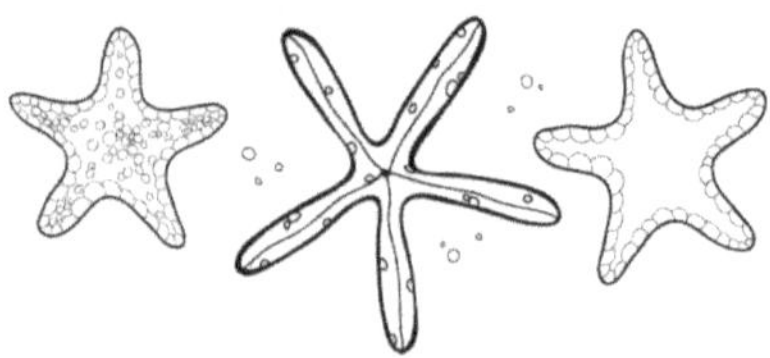

"**W**atch your..." Ouch. That had to hurt. The two chairs in his hands clatter down the rest of the steps to the foyer.

"Head? You were going to say head, weren't you?" Jake Prince, my brother, found the one doorway that challenges his six-foot-seven height. That it appears in a stairwell doesn't help.

My poor, clumsy, darling little brother. We Prince siblings really must be more careful of our noggins.

"Yeah. Apparently sometime in the past the stairs were re-routed, making the little turn shorter than average. You're the first person who's had a problem with it." He doesn't appreciate my cheesy grin OR my sense of humor. "I hope it doesn't leave a mark. Lydia would never forgive me."

He walks over to let me look at the mar on his forehead. "Don't worry. The bruise and bandage will be so high up nobody will notice."

"Very funny." I rub the spot with my finger, and then pat him on the arm. "You'll live."

"Where do you want these?" He gestures to the two wicker

rockers that preceded him down the steps. "These aren't for our wedding, are they?"

"Don't worry; they'll get a paint job before you see them again." He looks relieved. They are rather ratty, but a small vignette in the back of the chapel will be perfect for a photo op or a place for guests to sit for a moment. "I'm thinking white."

"Sounds perfectly bridal," he quips.

"That's the look I'm goin' for. Put them outside the front door for now. I'll have to wait for the calm to paint them." If Ms. Bertie were still next door, she would insist I paint them inside her fenced garden where the wind wasn't such a problem. I dare not with Marc working on his manuscript. Things between us are better, and I'd prefer to keep it that way and not push my luck.

"How are things with your neighbor?" Jake stood on the second rung of the ladder as I handed him light-bulbs. After my spill, ladders and I didn't gee-haw, and I would have been nearly all the way up there to do what Jake can practically do from a chair. Disgusting.

"Okay for now. I think he must be out of town. He hasn't harassed me in a few days."

Jake laughs. "I met him the other day. I think he guessed who I was."

"Not many in these parts as tall as you. He was at home when we were looking at the garden planning the reception. He never comes out when I'm with a client."

"How come?"

"I'm not sure. He's a little reclusive."

"Hmm. Wonder if he's always been that way." Jake climbs down the ladder and moves it to the next light fixture. "Seems like a nice enough guy."

"Pretty driven, from what I can figure out." I didn't mean to let my sigh out quite so loudly.

"What?" Jake tilts his head down to look at me.

"I know people think I'm not driven enough."

"What does it matter what 'people' think?"

I shrug my shoulder and make a big deal out of opening the second hermetically-sealed package of specialty light-bulbs. "I'm sure Mom and Dad, and lots of other people, think I should have stayed in banking."

"Anybody who thinks it's any of their business what you do for a living needs to worry about themselves." He stops, forcing me to look up at him. "And that includes our parents. You're doing something creative, and you help others. You're not the first person to leave a lucrative job to follow a call. You do realize you are good at everything you do?"

My lips curve in a grin, and I hope he doesn't see the tears gathering in my eyes. "You may be a little prejudiced. Thanks, Jakey. Because I couldn't go back if I wanted to. I just couldn't."

He nods his head. "I had a feeling there was more to it than simply tiring of working in finance."

"Yes, but I don't want to talk about it. Not now, anyway."

"Any time you're ready, I'm here. I may be your little brother, but you've always been pretty much my best friend."

Okay, that did it. The tears spill over and I have to hug him. "I love you, little bro." I pull back and shake my head. "Do you know how long I prayed for a younger sibling?"

"Apparently at least eight years."

The giggle makes its way out of my mouth and puts a smile on my face. "At least." I pull his face down to kiss him on the cheek. "And I think my prayers must have been pretty good."

# CHAPTER SEVEN

Two weeks. Jake and Lydia's wedding would be happening. Here.

The Stafford/Brundage wedding had gone off without a hitch. As I walk through, in my mind, what would happen the day of Jake's wedding, I catch a glimpse of movement in Ms. Bertie's yard – okay, Marc's yard. I haven't seen him in well over a week. I walk over to the window by my desk and notice he's wandering aimlessly through the garden, and his beard was quite a bit thicker than the last time I saw him. Does he look pale? Concern for my fellow man, okay for THIS man, makes me go to the door and open it to the garden.

I raise my hand, ready to greet him, when he looks up and sees me in the doorway. "Marc?"

He looks haggard. Simply downtrodden. Heartbroken?

"Are you all right?"

He gave me a sad half-grin and raises his hand in greeting. "Hi Chelsea. Yeah. I'm fine."

I gave him "the look." You know the one that says, "I'm frowning because I'm concerned and I don't believe you when you say 'I'm fine.'"

He recognizes it. He must have a mother, sister – oh, he certainly had a grandmother who used that look, and often used it on me.

"Really. I'm okay. Just tired."

"I haven't seen you in over a week. I figured you were out of town." There. That should get him talking.

He walks over to my stoop and gestures for me to have a seat, then sits beside me. "I've been in Columbia for a few days."

I glance around, looking for a wagging tail and a friendly 'woof,' finding neither. "Did you take Muffin with you? I could have taken care of her for you."

He sat, looking over the garden, taking a deep breath. Something has happened. When he turns to look at me, I can see the sadness in his eyes. "Muffin's gone, Chelsea."

No. Don't tell me Muffin's gone. Not like that. She's just displaced. "What? Did she run away? Is she living somewhere else?" I know the truth by the look on his face, but I don't want to know. Tears spring to my eyes as I shake my head.

He puts his arm around me. This is new. "Muffin had cancer."

I turn to look at him, pressing my hand to the ache in my chest that is more troubling than when I fell off the ladder. "No. Not Muffin, too. She can't be gone, gone."

"She is." He pulls his arm away, leaving me feeling cold in the South Carolina sunshine. "Last Saturday she couldn't get up, and I took her to Dr. Shemwell. There wasn't anything he could do. It was in her brain, and it hit her suddenly. Her symptoms up to then weren't any more than any dog of her age."

"She was fifteen." I whisper the words before putting my head down on my arms that were crossed on my knees. I can't keep the sobs inside. It's too much. First the man I trust violates my trust and disrupts my life, and then Ms. Bertie goes and dies on me, and now Muffin? When will it stop? The hurt so deeply and intricately embedded in my heart lashes out and engulfs me in its web. "It's too much."

Marc put his arm back around me, pulling me toward him as I attempt to stop crying. "I know. I didn't realize how attached to her I had become."

I sniff loudly and look up into his eyes. "She was a special dog. When I first moved out here, I think your grandmother would send her over here to keep me company. She worried that I was lonely." I pull a tissue from my pocket and blow my nose. It wasn't going to be enough, I could already tell.

"Here" He hands me a handkerchief.

This surprises me. "You carry a hankie?" It also slows the tears.

"I do. Granny told me a gentleman always has a handkerchief in his pocket so he can offer it to a lady in distress."

His sad grin almost did me in again.

"Your granny was an amazing woman. I don't know what I would have done without her." I thought back to the times I could talk to her the way I didn't dare talk to my own family. They would have been too hurt, on my behalf, to be able to simply listen to the ravings of a heart-broken girl without giving opinions and advice, however well-meant.

"Your family seems pretty close." He looks at me quizzically.

I straighten up and face him quickly. "Oh, we are, but there are some things I couldn't tell my family." I shake my head, convincing myself of the choice I'd made to keep my troubles to myself. "They wouldn't understand." I'd probably said too much.

He ponders a moment, looking at me. Looking straight into my eyes. For some reason, it isn't awkward. I simply stare back. What makes Marc McCallum tick?

"I get it." His gaze is focused in the direction of his house for a few seconds, then back at me. "Would you care to go for a walk on the beach?"

30

# CHAPTER EIGHT

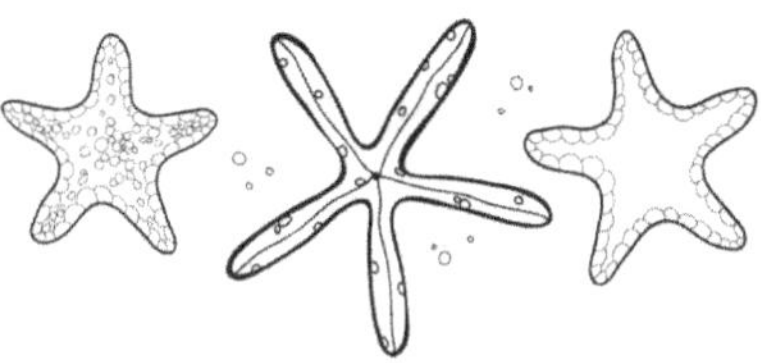

ears finally spent, I find myself feeling normal being alone around a man, family excepted, for the first time since Daniel.

"How is your book coming?" We had walked without talking for about five minutes. It wasn't a weird silence, but it was beginning to feel awkward.

He pauses, and then looks down at me with an eyebrow quirked. "Would you believe me if I said 'fine?'"

"Probably not."

We walk on, staring straight ahead, until he stops to face me, stuffing his hands in his pockets.

"I'm blocked."

"Blocked? As in 'writer's block?'"

He nods his head in the affirmative. "I haven't been able to write a word – not a good one, anyway – since I got here."

"That can't be good. Don't writers have deadlines?"

He glanced at the ocean behind me and nodded again. "I've always been able to crank out at least two thousand words a day, but now, I just sit there, looking at the blank screen. Or I write something, and then delete it because it stinks."

I stand there, considering what he's telling me. This man, the one who had gotten my dander up from day one, was reaching out to me for help. Me? Help? Here I am, feeling as though I have nothing to give, that everything is being taken away from me, and Marc is looking to me for advice.

I ponder before speaking. "I assume two thousand words is a lot?"

He quirks his lips in a rueful grin. "It's a first draft of a novel in less than two months."

"Oh. Wow. I had no idea." I thought it took a year – or five – to write a book? Something else is going on, obviously. "What's different this time?"

He stands there, a tiny line between his brows as he ponders my question. As if he really doesn't know what is different this time.

I give him a sidelong glance. "Do you have any ideas?"

Raking his hands through his hair, he sighs. "Honestly, I'm not sure. Losing Granny, and then Muffin didn't help. Or maybe I'm missing something. Maybe I'm washed up. A has-been. Maybe I need to concentrate on teaching and forget writing. It would certainly be easier." He turns and starts striding down the beach, hands stuffed in his pockets.

I run to catch up with him, then keep pace with his long strides by taking extra steps now and then. Walking in silence, Marc seems to come to himself when we get about a mile down the beach to the Sea View Inn.

He stops and turns to me, grinning sheepishly when he notices my red face. "I'm sorry. I didn't mean to drag you out here and wear you out. I'm sure you had other things planned for your day."

I'm a little surprised. This man who had irritated me from the get-go is worming his way into my good graces. How could this happen? Do I feel sorry for him? "I was ready for a break."

"You seem to work all the time."

"Feeling guilty, man of leisure?" I elbow him as we turn to walk back the way we came. When my arm comes in contact with him, I almost freeze. What am I doing? Flirting? Please, God, tell me I'm not flirting, because I do NOT want to be in a relationship. Not now, at any rate. Isn't part of my calling to find him a mate, for Ms. Bertie?

He chuckles and glances over at me, then stops when he sees my face. "Are you okay?"

"I'm fine." I drag my eyes up in his general direction, wincing a bit when I see he's still looking at me, eyes narrowed. "All right, I'm not fine, but I'm okay. How's that?"

"Better."

We walk on, both of us seeming to relax a bit.

"Nice day for a walk." I can't stand the silence anymore, so I break it. "I'm glad you suggested it."

Grinning, he nods. "We should do this again sometime."

"Yeah. Sometime."

# CHAPTER NINE

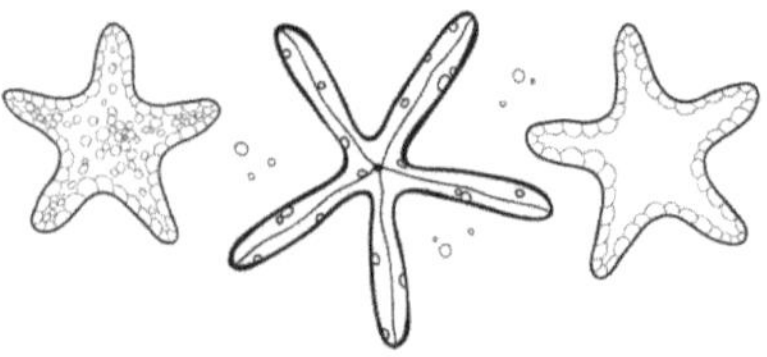

Working in the garden isn't the same without Muffin sniffing around and keeping me company. No wet nose working its way under my arm for a hug. No happy bark when I come through the door of the chapel into the walled garden.

Marc and I haven't gone for any more walks, and I wonder if we ever will. My anger is gone. For some reason, learning that he was trying to overcome obstacles like I was made him seem more...Well, more human?

Ms. Bertie had built Marc up in my mind to the point that when I finally met him, after the funeral, I was crushed to learn this ideal specimen of manhood from the photographs and his own grandmother's tales was just a man. An aggravating man, at that. After Daniel, I wanted to believe there were these ideal men out there waiting for a great girl like me. To learn that even the best guy was still just a GUY brought me down a notch. Maybe I spend so much time looking at the "happily ever after" that I don't recognize "normal." Or maybe this was my new normal.

Maybe neighbor Marc and I were destined to be grouchy old

people, living next door to one another, growing old alone and childless, neither of us having found "the one." If this is what God has for me, then so be it. I can handle it. Can Marc? Most men can't.

The garden is perfect. The perennials Ms. Bertie and I planted earlier are coming into their own, and the hydrangeas are going to be perfect for Jake and Lydia's wedding.

"Hey lady, did you order a pickup-truck of mulch?"

I look up to see my brother's goofy smile in the doorway of the chapel. "I did. Did you get bags or a load?"

"I got bags. Thought it would be easier to wheel in."

"Awesome. Pull the truck to the gate on the street, and we can bring it in through there."

"Gotcha."

He goes back into the chapel and outside to pull the truck around and Lydia comes bouncing through the door, her hair freshly-streaked with purple.

"Love the hair!" I jump up to hug her, which she returns gladly.

"Thanks! Charly was surprised that I wanted a fresh streak for the wedding, but you know me. I have a look."

"You do, and I love it. Someday I may surprise everyone and get a streak, too."

She laughs out loud. "Then people will REALLY get us confused."

"True." Jake comes in the gate, wheelbarrow groaning under the weight of four bags of mulch.

"Over-achiever." I pull one bag off and toss it where it needs to go. The low purr of a sports car made my head turn back to Lydia. "Who's that?"

"Charly and Rance. My matron-of-honor didn't want to be done out of any of it, so I told her they were welcome to help on mulching detail."

I shake my head as the couple come through the gate dressed for gardening. "Good thing she's a country girl at heart."

"Yeah, she is. And I think Rance is learning to be." Lydia rushes to her best friend, Charly, and gives her a hug. "Rance, what has she gotten you into this time?"

"Yet another opportunity to spend quality time together." He winks at his wife and pulls her close.

Charly beams back at her new husband. "Yes, and I figure the more males we have, the less lifting the females will have to do."

Rance clutches at his chest and groans. "Cut to the heart. I guess we're good for something, after all, eh Jake?"

Seeing the newlyweds together and their banter makes me long for something. What, I'm not sure, but it seems right, somehow.

I lean down to pick up a bag of mulch when I feel a tap on my shoulder.

"Here, let me help." Marc pulls off the second bag and puts it on the ground past where I had placed the first one. "How about you ladies give us instructions, and we men will take care of the heavy lifting."

I blink at him in surprise. "What are you doing? We have a deal, remember? I take care of the garden in exchange for using it."

"Maybe I'm considering re-thinking our deal." He quirks an eyebrow at me and grins. "It is, after all, my garden. If I want to help with the mulch, you can't stop me."

"If you put it that way..." I shrug my shoulders.

"I do. No way are you guys going to have all the fun."

"Mulch...fun." I shake my head in wonder. "How is it I've never put those two things in the same sentence before? Oh yes, I have. As in 'Spreading mulch is no fun when you get bits of mulch all over you."

Jake calls out. "Hey, Sis, you do realize it's not as bad for tall people."

"And how is that? I get it in every nook and cranny. Literally." I frown at my brother.

He winks at me and waggles his eyebrows at Marc. "We stay above it all."

I try to refrain from rolling my eyes at my little brother, and instead turn to Marc. "Have you met Charly and Rance?"

Marc takes his glove off and extends it. "We've met. Good to see you Dr. Butler, Charly."

"Call me Rance, please. I mean, after all, how can I have 'mulch fun' if we stand on ceremony?" His blue eyes really do twinkle when he smiles.

Groaning and laughter ensues as we all get to work, Jake, Marc, and Rance hauling, Lydia, Charly, and I spreading. We make quick work of it, and as we sit back on the ground, admiring our handiwork, I know I'm smiling.

"You look awfully pleased with yourself." Marc catches my attention with his words.

Shifting my gaze to him, he seems to have been watching me as I surveyed my – well his – domain. I lean forward, sitting cross-legged on the grass. "I am. It's exactly what Ms. Bertie and I envisioned." I look over at Lydia and Jake. "She was excited about your reception being here."

"That's sweet." Lydia looks a little misty as she leans her head on her fiancé's shoulder. "I'm glad we could help out."

Charly sighs. "Me, too. It's so peaceful. The fountain is such a nice touch."

"You know, it was while we were talking about Lydia and Jake's wedding that Ms. Bertie decided to get the fountain fixed." The antique iron fountain trickles happily in the center of the garden, making it an oasis on the hottest South Carolina day.

"I wondered. It never worked in my memory." Marc had leans back on his hands, his long, tan legs stretching out in front of him, feet crossed. "It was one of those things we got used to not working."

"I think that's why she was excited to work with me. It gave her a reason to bring this garden back to its original purpose, which was to be an oasis. And it certainly has been, for me."

Marc turns his head back toward me. "And for me."

# CHAPTER TEN

"Mom, your dress is stunning." I shake my head in wonder when I see my cute little mother standing there looking like an aging model. Her burgundy dress fit perfectly, and the shoe selection has begun.

She sighs. "Thank you, sweetie." She turns in the triple mirror trying to see the shoes from every angle. "I'm not sure about these. What do you think?"

I glance over at the stack of shoe boxes and frown in confusion. "How many pairs of shoes have you bought?"

Reddening slightly, she puts her hand to her mouth in a slight giggle. "Twelve." She holds her hand out when I would have spoken. I know my eyes are round as saucers. "Don't worry, they can all be returned. I wanted to try them all with the dress."

I laugh with her. "I understand. And nothing like waiting until three days before the wedding of your only son to make up your mind." I shake my head. "Oh, Mom, what if you don't pick any of them?"

She arched a well-plucked brow at me. "Don't worry. I will choose from these. They all fit, and they all meet the criteria, so if I don't find the perfect match, I'll find a pair that works."

"Good." I stand there, finger tapping on my chin. "I like those awfully well."

"Let's try another pair." She kicks those off and I pick them up and put them in the correct box.

The burgundy satin sling-back pumps with patent leather heels match her dress perfectly. "Oh wow."

"That's what I say. Wow." We both stand there, looking at her reflection in the mirror. Mom looks at me and nods. "These are the ones."

I nod in agreement. "I agree. They're perfect." I look at the ten unopened boxes. "What about all these?

"I've tried them all in the store, and I choose these. The others can go back."

"Let me look at them. I still need shoes to go with my dress."

Thankful my mother and I wear the same size shoe, I open the other boxes. When I see the platforms, I hold one up and cut a glance at her. "Really, Mom? You thought about these?"

She grins at me. "They remind me of some shoes I had when your dad and I started dating." She laughs as she looks at them closer. "I can't imagine walking down the aisle in them, though. What was I thinking?"

I slip them on, reveling in the extra height they give me. "You were thinking these would be perfect for your daughter, perhaps?" I walk around in them, and up to my mother, finally eye-to-eye with her. "Can I afford these?"

"I think we can work something out."

"Looks like a trip to the mall next week."

She nods and preens in front of the mirror a few more minutes. "That'll be fun. We'll be ready to relax and eat ice cream by then."

"Still dieting, huh?"

"Definitely. I'm not going to mess it up now. I don't think this dress would be very forgiving if I gain any weight now." She winks at me. "Your dad says I look twenty years younger."

"Watch it. I don't want you catching up with me."

"Don't worry. You'll look twenty all your life, I figure. Me? I looked twenty-five when I was fifteen. My dad, on the other hand, always looked young, like you."

"I've found it's not a bad thing. Maybe I won't get tagged as an 'old maid' too soon." I sigh and take the shoes off and put them carefully back in the box.

"With those shoes, you definitely won't look like an old maid." Mom looks at me intently, her attention off her reflection and on to mine. "You've got time, and God's got the right man for you. It's all about His timing, not ours."

"Exactly, and if He decides I need to be alone and take care of these young whipper-snapper couples, that's okay, too." I nod confidently, refusing to meet my mother's eyes in the mirror.

"Is it really?"

I glance up to see her scrutinize me. Why I feel tears threaten is beyond me. Maybe I'm emotional because Jake is getting married. It has to be "sympathy tears" for my mom. But she's not crying, I am.

# CHAPTER ELEVEN

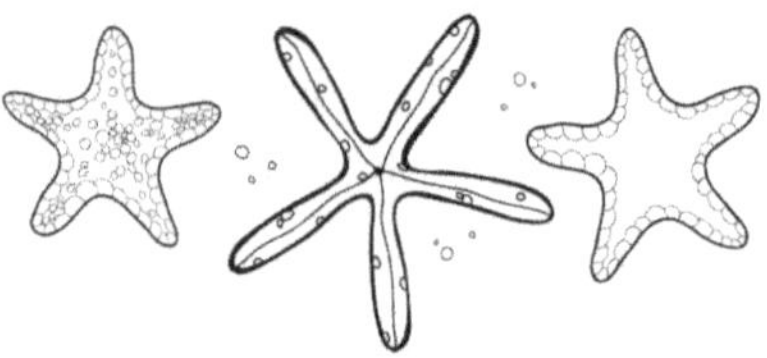

*L*iving next door to your venue has its advantages. When Ms. Bertie suggested using her garden for recep- tions, it was a God-send. I didn't want to ask, but she offered.

Feeling pretty good about the progress made in preparing for Jake's wedding, I glance out the window by my desk and notice Marc sitting on his patio, laptop in front of him. I like seeing him there, working. He's tapping away. Maybe his writing block is over. He looks up and sees me in the window, raises a hand, and grins in my direction. I wave back, and a warm fuzzy feeling comes over me I can't explain. I feel myself smile, and I look down at my "to do" list and realize this has been one of the smoother weddings I've hosted. When I look back to where Marc was sitting, I see the empty chair and the thought enters my mind I haven't done anything toward finding the right woman for my neighbor.

Then another fleeting thought enters my mind: I'm happy.

I haven't thought about Daniel in at least a week. I look up again to see Marc striding across the yard toward the chapel, and wonder when I feel a little leap in my chest. The side door is open to the old-fashioned screen door to let in the ocean breeze, and I hear a gentle knock. "Anybody home?"

"Come on in. The door's unlatched."

He strides up the step and into the door. "How's it going?" He has an eager look on his face – much different from the look he generally wore when first we met.

"Honestly, it's going well enough that I'm super-afraid I've forgotten something vital. Know what I mean?"

He laughs, a hearty, pleasant sound. "I know exactly what you mean. During school months, if I feel that way I've usually missed a deadline or have a stack of compositions I've forgotten to grade. Pride goeth before a fall."

"Exactly." I close the folder in front of me. "How's the book coming? I noticed you over there working away. I've tried to keep from distracting you."

He flickers a look toward me with a half-grin. "I've finally been inspired. And don't worry about distracting me. I'm beginning to think you may be my muse."

"Really? Hmmm. Maybe inspiration isn't as finicky as you thought?" I couldn't help but let the chuckle loose, reminding him of the conversation we had, weeks ago, about that very fact. He had convinced himself, then, that inspiration was a fickle taskmaster requiring peace and quiet.

I see his face redden slightly at the memory. "I may have overstated it a bit. Sometimes I think I'm more fearful of distractions than is merited." He shrugs his shoulder. "Maybe there's more to inspiration than guaranteeing peace and quiet. Anyway, I've decided there are some distractions worth seeking."

"Such as?" I raise my eyebrows, wondering what in the world he's thinking.

"Such as a walk along the beach with a lovely lady." He lifts his own eyebrows in question.

I begin to chew on my lips. The last time we walked together on the beach was when Muffin had died, and we were both grieving for her. We shared things that day we'd never re-visited. I look up into his face, looking for traces of Daniel, and I don't see it. I don't see any of the things that make me distrust men -- or at least one type of man in particular. His countenance is clear, his smile, genuine.

"Might be the last chance you have until after your brother's wedding." Eyebrows lifted, he looks at me intently.

"Are you trying to distract ME?" A smile gurgles up into a laugh, and when he holds out his hand, I take it willingly.

"Maybe I am."

And maybe I'll find him a woman another day.

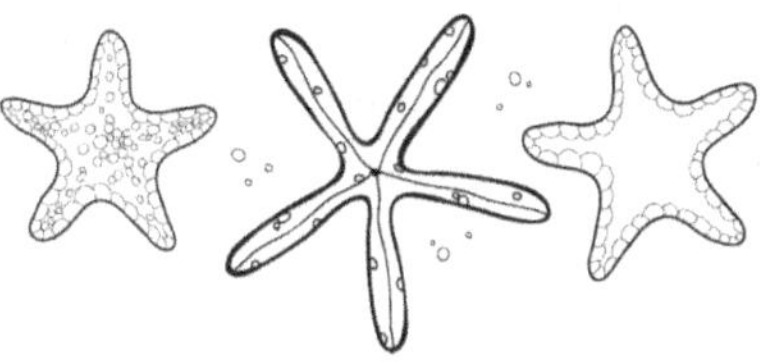

It never fails. If you want your hair to blow with your part, you're going the wrong direction. Always.

Marc didn't have much to say once we began walking on the beach, but I didn't either. For some reason I felt shy. Like I was a teenager crushing on the captain of the football team. I don't want to crush on Marc. I want to be happy and on my own and...I glance up at him and see a slight grin on his face.

"Penny for them?" I have to ask. His grin was turning slightly goofy, and I certainly didn't want him asking what I am thinking about.

He startles slightly, looking at me in surprise. "For my thoughts?"

I prop a hand on my hip. "No, for your back yard, silly."

"That would solve everything, wouldn't it?" He quirked an eyebrow at me and chuckled.

"Maybe. Jake's wedding is the last one on the list before you get to decide my fate." My air quotes around 'decide my fate' made him smile.

"Sounds ominous." He stops and looks off into the distance before turning to face me.

"It feels a little ominous." I scrutinize him as he stops in front of me on the beach. There aren't many people out today, being a weekday. Mostly retirees and a few moms with small children digging in the sand.

"I wouldn't worry. Our deal is working out fine as far as I'm concerned."

Relief. And something else I can't quite name. "I'm glad to hear I haven't been too much of a distraction." He's still standing there, looking at me.

"My editor called me this morning."

"Trying to hurry up the muse?"

He stuffs his hands deep in the pockets of his shorts and looks off toward the water, smiling. He looks back at me and shrugs. "No, to tell me he loves the new story. I sent him three chapters last night."

"That's great! See, I told you my business wouldn't be a nuisance." I fake-punch him in the chest, and he fake-feints as he grabs my hand.

"He told me there is a spark in my writing he hasn't seen before."

He still holds onto my hand, and I feel my insides begin to quiver. Fear? Confusion? Anticipation? I have to talk. If we keep talking, I'll relax. I clear my throat nervously. "How do you account for it?"

"A couple of things. One, I think God finally has me where He wants me. I've spent time with Him, which has been in short supply in the last few years. Two, I think I've spent too long pushing the world away. Life is going on all around me, and I've just started to appreciate it. I never write drafts during the school year when I'm teaching. Too many distractions. I'll edit, but not write, per se. I wonder if that's been a mistake."

I tilt my head to look up into his face. "Sometimes it's easier that way."

I've done the same thing. Rather than admit I was afraid of

relationships, I opted out. I clung to my family and a few close friends, and pushed others away.

He shakes his head. "It's easier, but not in the long run. Ultimately, God doesn't want a bunch of lone wolfs. He wants his children to act like a family."

"And none of us are 'only children' in His family." I turn my hand in his and squeeze. "You make a good point."

He pokes his chest with his thumb. "I'm a writer. I get paid to make good points."

"Then you're in the right business." We turn and continue our stroll, this time hand-in-hand. "What's your story about, or is that information classified?"

He turns to look down at me and smiles. "It's a historical novel about a young widow on the coast of Scotland who has captured the attention of a local Laird. The McCallums are Scottish, you know."

For a moment I forget to blink. "Are you writing...romance?" I've looked up his work on Amazon. He writes historical novels, yes, but romantic novels? Not before now, anyway.

He tilts his head and a confused frown crosses his face. "Romance? Of course not..." He pauses, bringing us both to a stop as he looks at me with what I can only call slight horror. "Chelsea."

I am trying desperately to stop the laughter from bubbling up. "Marc. What's wrong?"

"I think I'm writing a historical romance novel." He rakes his free hand over his face as he shakes his head in disbelief.

I tug at his hand, still enveloping mine. "Hey."

I pause for him to look at me. When he does, I grin at him, still holding in the giggle that wants to escape. "If I'm your muse, at least I'm not inspiring you to write a horror novel."

# CHAPTER THIRTEEN

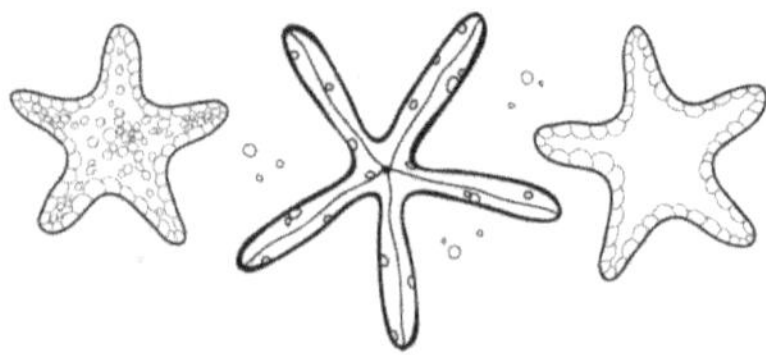

"*B*eautiful." I can't help but sigh with pleasure at the small sanctuary of the Pawleys Island Wedding Chapel. The "shabby chic" pews of different vintages, whitewashed to match, were perfect. Every other pew end, on the aisle, ribbon holds a paper cone with stems of hydrangea, dusty miller, and gardenia softening the effect of the mis-matched furnishings.

The scent of gardenia could be overpowering, but with the windows open to the ocean breeze, it is a mixture of aromas that spell summer in the south.

For myself, I prefer the old-fashioned orange blossoms. But it's not about me this time. It's about Lydia and Jake. Those pesky tears tend to pop out again, but I promised myself when I took on my baby brother's wedding that I would not be the silly old-maid-sister who couldn't stand the thought of her lil' bro getting married to "that woman." Lydia is exactly who I would have picked for Jake a wife, if I could have picked. That I missed out on most of their dating and courtship made me have regrets that have no place in this weekend.

Because it's not about me.

I hear a ding from my phone and see a text message.

I feel my face blanch when I recognize the number. Daniel. I cleared his number out of my contacts when we parted, so at least his name and face won't come up anymore. But I know that number. I should have blocked it.

"Chels, I'm coming to Pawleys. I want to see you. Give me a few minutes, whenever you say. Be there tomorrow through next week."

No. I would not see him. Hasn't he done enough to pull me down, to denigrate my confidence? I am finally at a good place in my life. I have friends. I have a job I love. I may not have romance, but unless it's "the one," it's highly over-rated, if you ask me.

The soft rapping on the side door to Ms. Bertie's garden – though Marc lives there, it will always be Ms. Bertie's garden – rouses me from my sinking thoughts. Is it Marc? I rush to the screen door to see Emmaline and Rafe Jernigan at the door. I feel slight disappointment and cover it quickly with a smile. At least I can put off answering Daniel -- or deciding whether or not TO answer Daniel.

"Hi! Come in -- or should I come out?"

Emmaline, the creative genius of this wedding, bestows one of her gracious smiles. "Come on out and see what you think. We're still at 80 guests, right?"

"We are." As we walk toward the magical arrangement of tables, textiles, lights, and greenery, I have to shake my head in wonder. "Emma, it is amazing."

"I thought the string lights would add a nice touch as the sun goes down, don't you?" The cafe lights went from post to tree, to another tree, to a hook on the chapel, and back to the beginning.

"It's beautiful. I know they will be thrilled. I hope I can keep them away until the reception. I want them to be surprised." I cross my arms across my chest and look around with satisfaction, my anxiety over Daniel's message melting away in the beauty that was my gift to my little brother and his beautiful bride. "They've been determined to pay for everything themselves."

Emma nodded. "I've kept some of the details to myself, so fingers-crossed that they keep their noses out of the garden until after the ceremony." She points to the head table. "You were right. Those over-sized candlesticks were perfect for the head table."

"I agree." I glance at Emma's proud husband. "Rafe, what did Emma do before you came along?"

He laughs. "She hired a crew of guys to move stuff around. Now she tells me where things go, and I end up moving them around until it's perfect."

Emma tucked her hand into the crook of his arm. "In reality, he gets it right a lot quicker than anyone else, so I've come to depend on him more than I should, probably."

"You can depend on me for anything. You know that." He kisses his wife on her beautifully coiffed red hair.

"I know." Her smile, always beautiful, was dazzling when turned to her husband. It made me happy being with them, knowing there were couples depending on one another for physical help, and encouragement as well. For better or worse, isn't that in the wedding vows?

I know Emma was a widow for several years before she remarried, and Rafe had been a bachelor. They seem happy and content together, although I'm sure there have been hurts in their past that made it difficult to trust again. I can't imagine losing a spouse and raising a daughter on my own.

"Rafe, Emma, how are you?" Marc stops beside me and puts an arm around my shoulder, which somehow I do not mind. This is a first for me. "Chelsea?"

I smile up at him. "I'm good. Ready to get this wedding going."

"I hear that." He chuckles and looks at Rafe and Emma. "I

would have come out and helped with the tables and chairs, but I was at a spot in my manuscript where I couldn't stop without losing steam."

"Hey, anybody that can write a whole book, completely thought up out of his own head, is excused from grunt work." Rafe laughed and shook his hand.

"Unless there is mulch involved." I hold up a finger and look at him with a grin.

"Definitely when there is mulch. Many hands make light work, though, and I'll be available all day tomorrow for whatever you need."

I tilt my head back and look at him, feeling a sheen of moisture in my eyes. "Thank you, Marc. That means a lot."

He shrugs his shoulders. "That's what neighbors are for, isn't it?"

"Yes, well…" Emmaline looks at her husband and winks. "Good neighbors are hard to find, I hear."

Please let me not blush. Please. Please. Please. Nope, I feel the heat rising on my face. I may be a brunette, but my fair skin seems to be in league against me when it comes to blushing. Daniel hated when I blushed.

"Hon, we need to get home and get you fed." Patting her hand resting on his arm, Rafe winks at his wife, causing her to blush. At least I'm not alone. Redheads blush too, apparently.

She looks at her watch and then smiles up at him. Yes, we do." She involuntarily placed her hand on her abdomen. A clue if ever there was one.

I look my friend straight in the eye. "Emma…Is there something we should know?"

She looks at Rafe, who nods, then back at me. "We found out last week."

"You're…"

"We're pregnant!" Rafe spills it with alacrity. "We're not

telling it until we're a little further along, so let's keep it on the down-low."

"Does Sophie know?" The gooseflesh on my arms has gooseflesh, I'm so excited.

"Oh yes, and she's over the moon." Emma grinned. "I was afraid she would be embarrassed, a teenager acquiring a baby brother or sister, but she is thrilled."

"Oh, Emma, this is wonderful." I can't help it. I have to hug them both. "You'll be such great parents."

"We may be in wheelchairs by the time he or she gets out of high school, but I can't wait. My first child at almost fifty years old. Ten years ago I would have been afraid to have a child call me 'dad.'"

"Ten years is a long time, Rafe." Emma slips her arm around her husband's waist and hugs him. "It's what we are now that is important."

"Amen." He winks at his wife and sniffs, suspicious moisture in his eyes as he smiles.

"Congratulations, you two. We'll keep it quiet until you're ready to announce it, but I'll be watching you, Emmaline." Marc shook a finger at her face. "No taking chances when you're in my garden. Between Rafe and me, we'll be there to lift and pull anything you need."

When he looks over at me, I notice there might be a slight dewiness in Marc's eyes, as well.

# CHAPTER FOURTEEN

he dress chosen by myself and Lydia for my bridesmaid dress is beautiful. I turn in my three-panel mirror, checking to make sure the shoes work. Mom has great taste in shoes, even if she can't wear them. The platforms and the flowing chiffon print are perfect together. I've got to get changed for the rehearsal dinner at Bistro 217. This is the one event where I can simply enjoy being part of the wedding party.

I'm sliding the swingy cocktail dress over my head when I hear a knock. On the front door. I seldom hear knocks on the front door unless I have an appointment. I slip out the door of my studio apartment and sneak a peek out the sidelights of the double doors, and when I see who it is, I freeze.

It's Daniel. I decided to ignore his text, hoping he would get the message that I didn't want to see him. Apparently passivity, another thing he tended to berate me for, wasn't going to work. I should have known. I look up, tears gathering in my eyes, and pray. "God, why on earth is he here, and now of all times? Hasn't he hurt me enough?"

He knocks again, and almost immediately after, I hear a knock on my side door leading to Ms. Bertie's garden. Marc. I rush across the building, hoping Daniel didn't see a flash of azure blue silk in the sidelight.

I open the door, a smiling Marc on the other side, a bouquet of flowers in his hand. His smile dips when he sees my face. "Are you all right?"

"Yes. No." I close my eyes for a second and open the screen door for him to come in. "Honestly, I couldn't tell you. Someone's at the other door and I don't want to answer it."

"Who is it?"

"Daniel."

"Who is Daniel?"

"I dated him when I lived in Charlotte. We were...pretty serious."

"And you don't want to see him?" He looks at me closely. "You're pale, Chelsea, and you're crying."

"I feel pale." All the memories are flooding back. "I would have married him, Marc. Until..."

"He hurt you." Marc's eyes narrow, his face beginning to redden in anger.

His reaction gets my attention. He's angry on my behalf. "It was probably my fault. I didn't understand..."

"How about we answer the door. If you don't, he'll come back later." He hands me the flowers and puts his hand on my arm, guiding me to the door. "I'm right here."

"Why are you doing this?" How can he trust that I wasn't to blame? I mean, sometimes I, myself, feel I was to blame. I'm sure if I tell him exactly what happened, he will wonder if there wasn't something I could have done to stop Daniel's advances. Surely it was my fault that I took to heart his belittling and scolding in private. Surely I should have sucked it up and been the woman he wanted, instead of being stubborn about what I wanted. Surely?

"Because I have a sister."

Why did the fact that he equated me with a sister hurt almost as much as Daniel's slights?

He takes my hand and stops me before we get to the door. "And because you are important."

In looking into his eyes, I can see that I must have a smile blooming on my face, because he returns it and leans down to kiss my forehead. "Let's get this over with so we can get to the rehearsal dinner."

"You're going?" I'm completely at sea, now. I had no idea Marc and Jake had become such good friends.

He shrugs his shoulder and sends me a half-grin. "Apparently mulching and providing the reception space garners an invite to the rehearsal. I was hoping you'd go with me."

I put my nose down into the bouquet of flowers and smile up at him. "Thank you, Marc." I note the silence at the door and wince a little. "Do you think maybe he's gone?"

The knock answered my question.

"That's a no. Come on. I'll be your wing-man."

I take a deep breath and open the door. When Daniel turns toward me, I am amazed I have no feeling whatsoever. Other than gladness that Marc McCallum stood behind me like a sentinel.

"Daniel."

"Chelsea, I thought maybe you hadn't gotten my text."

"I did. I chose not to answer it." I feel the muscles in my shoulders begin to bunch until Marc's hand gently lands on my shoulder and squeezes. I look up at him and take strength from his steady gaze. "Come in. We were on our way out, but we can talk for a minute."

Daniel looks at Marc, and then back at me. "This is a private conversation, Chelsea."

"I'd like to introduce you to my neighbor, Marc McCallum. Marc, this is Daniel Rogers. We used to work together in Charlotte."

"Daniel. I've heard your name mentioned." Good save, Marc. He turns to me. "Would you like me to wait in the car?"

"No, anything Daniel has to say, he can say in front of you."

"Very well." He looks at Daniel and cocks his head a bit. "You heard the lady."

Daniel rubs the back of his neck nervously. I recognize the body language, something I should have noticed when we were dating. He's unsure of himself. I realize, now, with Marc standing stolidly behind me, that it was insecurity on his part, not anger with me that made him do the things he did that I took personally. My lack of confidence wasn't the problem, it was his perceived inadequacy that he blamed, erroneously, on me.

"Chels, I wanted to see you, to talk to you about how we left things."After hem-hawing around for a few seconds, he drew himself up and looked down at me.

What used to create fear in me now only irritates me. Whatever made me think I was in love with him? "How we left things? You mean how you constantly belittled me, physically attacked me, and when I didn't reciprocate you made it impossible to do my job?" Marc's hand squeezes tighter. I can tell his anger is rising, and not at me. "Daniel, you ruined my reputation at our place of work. Do you expect me to simply dismiss what you've done?"

"You always did take criticism too personally."His dismissive tone pours out the rest of the nervousness, and all I can feel is Marc's steady presence behind me in more ways than one.

I simply stare at him. "No, I don't think so. I think YOU try to make it all about YOU." I pause, giving him a chance to rebut, shaking my head as he simply stares at me as if I've grown two heads. "Does this behavior sound reasonable to you?"

Daniel's phone dings with a text message, and he lifts the phone to check it, frowning at me as if it's my fault. "I've got to go. This discussion isn't over. I think we should, as reasonable adults, be able to work this out. I still have feelings for you, Chels."

"Daniel, bless your heart, this discussion IS over. I am a reasonable adult, but it doesn't mean I have to be around people who undermine my confidence and hurt me. It's taken me this long to get to a good place in my life. A place where God is calling the shots, not you. I trust Him. You? I forgive you, but I don't trust you. I pray that someday you will learn to think of others before yourself."

I look up at Marc, and he winks at me. The power of God and Marc McCallum is a potent thing.

Daniel stands there, looking at me, dismissing Marc altogether. "If that's the way you want it, fine."

I would love to laugh in his face, but I still don't feel like laughing. "It is. And the next time you think about contacting me? Don't. I'll have your number blocked."

He quirks his eyebrow up sardonically. "There are other ways to find people."

Marc speaks up. "There is such a thing as a restraining order if she cares to file one."

Daniel looks up, surprised, as if he's forgotten the tall, quiet man standing behind me.

"I don't want to go to the trouble, but I can. I would hope, as a 'reasonable adult,' you will respect my wishes." I turn to Marc. "We need to go if we're going to be at the restaurant on time."

"Yes. So," he speaks directly to Daniel, "if you will excuse us, we need to be on our way. Ready, Darling?"

I give Marc my most brilliant smile, trying really hard to stifle the giddy laughter urging its way out. "Ready, Sweetheart."

# CHAPTER FIFTEEN

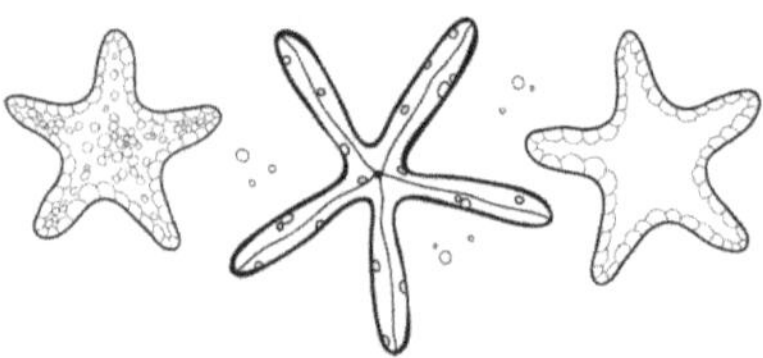

The rehearsal had gone perfectly, which was a bit worrisome, since in my experience a rough rehearsal makes for a perfect performance. I won't think about that now. The clouds on the horizon were concerning enough. What if it rains? Will the reception be ruined?

I hear a knock on the side door and rush to answer it, running my hands through my wild bed-head hair and making sure I am completely dressed. At this point in the day of the event, it could be anyone. I know who I hope it is.

Marc. I smile as I open the door and then push the screen out to let him enter.

"Hi. You okay this morning?" He's looking at me closely, I know, to see if the unwelcome encounter with Daniel had thrown me for a loop.

"I'm good. My baby brother is getting married today!" I reach up and hug him tightly, not thinking about what I'm doing. When he holds me close and squeezes, I realize I feel at home here. Am I so fickle as to think I'm in love with one man and then another so quickly? Whatever happened to my resolve to find him a wife, and to be content in my single-ness?

I release him and step back, putting my hands behind my back. "I'm sorry. I guess the excitement of the day has me a bit wound up."

Marc's eyes are gleaming as he smiles down at me. "No apology needed. Any time you feel the need to fling yourself in my arms, I think I can handle it." He lifts an eyebrow at me, making me laugh.

"Thank you. Your Granny Bert had the best hugs since my Grandma. Sometimes I need a good hug." Maybe that put him off the scent.

"If you need a Granny hug, I'll bring my Great-Aunt Prudie over."

I wrinkle my nose at him, knowing he's playing with me. "She does have good ones, too."

"What can I do to help today?" He gets down to business.

I wilt a little and whine. "Start praying for sunshine?"

"Already done, and I think I've got a solution."

"A solution to an outdoor venue in a rainstorm? One in which the cost-saving venue-provider didn't plan for a tent 'just in case?'" There's no way I would ask him to have the reception inside the house. I growl and put both hands in my hair in frustration.

"Yes."

I'm confused. "What do you mean, 'yes.'"

He grabs my elbows and pulls my hands out of my hair, then takes my hands. "I called Ken Hodge this morning and asked if he had a clear-top tent that would fit our space. I understand they're a thing."

"You know Ken?" I'm staring at him, unbelieving.

He shrugs. "I do. He's a distant relative – apparently we're related to almost everyone around here."

"Except for me."

A strange look crossed his face. "Please, Lord, I hope not."

I smack him on the chest, and he grabs my hand. "Finish your story."

"I called him; he's thrilled to help out. It should arrive within the hour, and I promised I would help set it up. That way you're covered -- no pun intended -- rain or shine."

"I could kiss you." My voice, I knew, was getting softer and softer, tears nearer and nearer. When had anyone outside of my dad and Jake ever cared for me like this?

"I could let you."

To my surprise, he does just that. His lips feather across my forehead, my cheek, and then rest on my lips. When I sigh, he pulls me closer.

Maybe Marc McCallum has a future in writing romance novels, after all.

# CHAPTER SIXTEEN

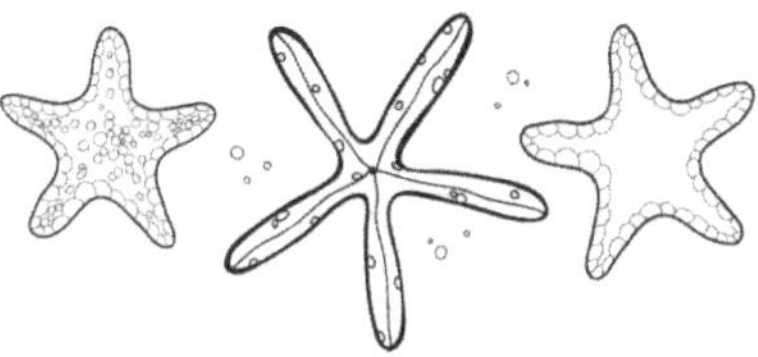

The pink roses scattered on my dress are no match for the color in my cheeks. Whether it is excitement about my brother's wedding or Marc's kiss is a toss-up. When have I ever felt this way?

Mom, a.k.a. the mother-of-the-groom, is beautiful in her new dress and heels. She and Lydia's mother are sitting in the white wicker chairs in the corner, a box of tissues on the table between them. The dads are standing in the other corner, hands in pockets, talking about the latest news and sports teams.

"Chelsea, do you have any safety pins?" Charly looks frantic. "Our flower girl stepped on her hem and ripped it a bit. Mari-Anne is crying, thinking she's ruined the wedding."

Four-year-old MariAnne, Charly's niece, is sitting in her dad's lap. Tom Livingston, the tall, robust chief of police, is comforting his little girl the way only a father can.

"Here, let me see." Emma to the rescue. "Chelsea, you go on up and help Lydia. I've got a sewing kit and I'll take care of it" She looks at me over her reading glasses that she will lose as soon as the wedding starts." You're part of the wedding party, you know."

"I know. I'm not used to being part of the event. I'm usually on 'help' detail."

Emma nods in understanding. "Scoot. Charly's taking care of the flower girl and ring bearer, so somebody needs to take care of the bride."

"Gotcha." I take one more look around, see that everything is in place, including Sarah Benton at the piano putting music in order.

"Chelsea..."

I laugh and raise my hands in surrender. "I'm going."

Since Lydia is family, I've allowed the bride and bridesmaids, which includes me, after all, to use my apartment to get ready. I'm glad I sprung for the triple department-store mirror when it was going out of business. Lydia is standing there, hand on her chest, staring at herself in the mirror. She sees my reflection behind her.

"Is this really me?" She whispers to me.

I stand next to her and put my arm around her waist. "It really is. You look gorgeous."

"I was tempted to grow out my hair for 'wedding hair,' but Jake didn't want me to."

I smile. "Jake's never known you with longer hair." The soft curls and the single blossom in her hair with the tiny birdcage netting is perfect for her. As petite as me and more so, the figure-hugging lace sheath with an attached chiffon train is non-traditional enough to be "her."

She tilts her head and smiles. "True." She looks at me. "You look beautiful, too."

"You chose well when you chose pink." I wink at her. Sisters already. "And it looks great on Charly."

"I was afraid hers wouldn't fit by the time the wedding rolled around." She laughed and tucked a curl back in place, grabbing the hairspray immediately after. Then she turns, hand to lips, her eyes round. "I wasn't supposed to say anything."

"Is she...?" There must be something in the water.

"She is." She looks up in time to see her matron-of-honor enter with the mothers of the bride and the groom.

"She is' what?" Charly narrowed her eyes at her best friend and bride. "Are you telling tales out of school?"

Lydia's mother chuckled warmly. "Hon, you can't keep secrets like that. Your mama and I figured it out before you did."

Charly waves a hand in dismissal as we all rush to hug her. "Why am I not surprised? Rance delivered my niece and nephew and was floored when I told him I was expecting. Not a clue."

Nothing compares to the laughter between women who come together for a joyous occasion. Lydia's getting married. Charly's pregnant with her first child.

Me? I was kissed this morning. That delicious little fact will stay under wraps for a while. Unless my mother gets a whiff of it. In the meantime, I giggle right along with them as if I'm simply joining in on their happiness, when all the time I'm thinking about a slightly scruffy beard and strong arms holding me and making me feel things I've never felt before.

# CHAPTER SEVENTEEN

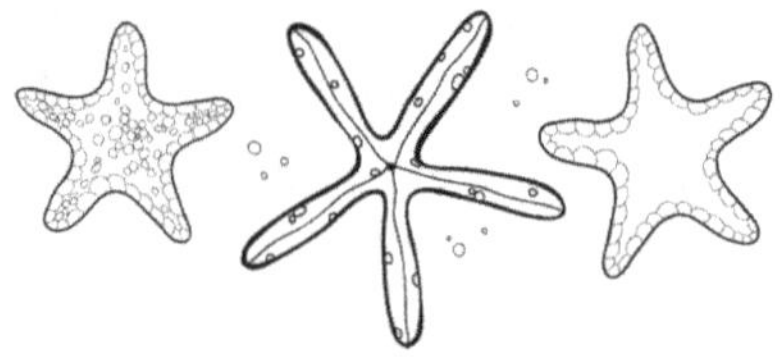

"All right people, it's time to get this show on the road." Emma claps her hands at the wedding party and parents standing on the front porch of the Pawleys Island Chapel. When she finally gets our attention, she smiles. "You all look perfect. Now, get in order. Groom's parents, bride's mother, then watch for the guys to come in from the side door. When they're in place, it'll be Chelsea, Charly, then you two sweeties," winking at an intent Evan and MariAnne," and then the main event -- Lydia."

Lydia raises her hand. "Do I have permission to pull that out next time Jake argues with me?"

After the laughter subsides, Emma nods. "Use it any time you need to. No guarantees, though." She looks at her watch. "It's two o'clock."

Lydia's dad raised a hand. "Can we pray first?"

Emma's smile is misty, as is everyone else's. "By all means."

He nods, then bows, holding the hand of his little girl. "Dear Heavenly Father, we offer up this day, and this couple, to you. They're your children. We were given care of them for a little while, and for that, we, the parents, are thankful. We love them, but we cannot fathom just how much You love them, and for that, we offer gratitude. Bless them, bless their lives as a new family in your sight, and bless those of us standing beside them. May we all feel the presence of Your Holy Spirit today. In Your great and mighty name we pray, Amen."

"Daddy, you promised you wouldn't make me cry, and now look at me." Lydia hugs her dad and Emma immediately hands her a tissue.

"You're fine. Investing in waterproof makeup was a good call." Emma takes the damp tissue and hands her a hankie. "Here's one to hold with your bouquet."

"Oh! I was going to get one of Granny's, but I forgot." Lydia's chin quivers.

"I've got you covered. Your mom handed it to me this morning. It was your granny's."

Lydia smiles. "Perfect. I've got one grandmother's pin, and one grandmother's hankie." She fingers the blue butterfly pin she'd always coveted from her mother's jewelry box." She takes a deep breath. "I'm ready."

After the pastor, Jake and the groomsmen -- Rance and Jake's friend, Matthew -- enter from the right, Marc steps up to my mother, mother-of-the-groom, and holds out his arm. "I've been pressed into service as an usher today. I hope you don't mind." He looks from my mother to me and back again.

She pats him on the arm. "I think it would be a good thing for us to get acquainted, don't you?" She sidles a glance at me and winks.

Marc looks over his shoulder and grins at me as I put my fingers to my lips and stifle a chuckle.

And they're off. I watch as Marc, handsome in his dark grey suit, escorts my mother to her seat. I see him lean in to hear something she says, and then answer her. She reaches up to kiss him on the cheek. What is that all about?

No time to think about myself. Lydia's mother is being escorted by her cousin, and then I'm up.

Standing at the doorway, Marc is standing straight and tall, taking his new responsibility as usher very seriously. "Careful in those heels. I've seen you on a ladder, you know."

I know my face is bathed in glorious color, which, once I get over being aggravated and aflutter at the same time, I know is a good thing. I lean toward him and whisper, "Wise guy." He quirks his eyebrow at me and winks, and I can't get the grin off my face as I make my way down the aisle. A random thought comes into my mind that in these shoes I'm only eight inches shorter than he.

Charly is next, glowing with a secret smile for which only a few know the reason. I glance over at her husband, Rance, and see moisture in his eyes that compliment his smile as he watches his wife make her way. I know they're both reliving their own wedding not quite a year ago.

The Livingston twins, tow-headed Evan and sunny blonde MariAnne, do their jobs perfectly as ring bearer and flower girl. I can see a spark of mischief on Evan's face as he makes his way slowly to the front, holding the ring on a pillow. MariAnne is carefully placing the rose petals at almost equidistant spaces, a tiny frown on her face as she concentrates on getting the spacing perfect. Twins, but so very different. Evan's exuberant personality definitely takes after his mother, Lucy, who is sitting on an aisle seat holding her breath until they both get up to the altar area. MariAnne? She is her daddy. Serious, meticulous, and always striving to do the right thing.

And now, the bride. My new sister. The love of my baby brother's life. Lydia's eyes glance at her dad's before they start, and then she locks them on Jake, her smile glorious. I look over at my brother, and what I see almost brings me to my knees. The love I see on his face, the tears beginning to fall from his lashes, are tributes of love for his new wife.

Maybe it's because I've never had anyone this close to me get married, or maybe it's because when I glance back at Lydia, my gaze wanders to the back doors and Marc. My feelings are mixed. It's a combination of excitement for the future, happiness for those around me, and a little fear. Fear that what I'm feeling won't last. Fear I'll discover something that breaks my heart, as it did with Daniel.

But when Marc smiles at me – and only me -- across the crowd from the back of the sanctuary, a sudden peace drives out all the fear.

# CHAPTER EIGHTEEN

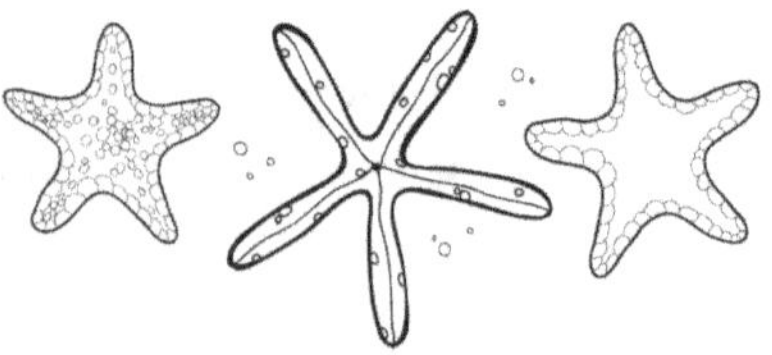

"How did you end up being an usher?"

Marc and I are standing on his patio, a little apart from the others, taking in the scene before us. Toasts have been made, laughter and jokes about the difference in Jake's and Lydia's heights are prevalent, and sweet tributes from the fathers of both the bride and groom have everyone, including myself, alternately laughing and crying.

Marc leans down to answer me. "One of Lydia's cousin's couldn't make it. Something about an abscessed tooth"

"Ouch!" I cringe as I think about it. "You did a great job. I was surprised, that's all."

"I have many talents, ushering weddings is only one of my many accomplishments."

"Always the usher, never the groom, eh?" I tuck my hand in his arm and he squeezes it close.

"Pretty much."

"I'm with you. I'm not 'Twenty-Seven Dresses' bridesmaid material, but I've got a fairly good collection." I look down at the gown I'm wearing today. "This one, on the other hand, is actually cute."

"Who picked it out?" He lifts an eyebrow at me.

"Well, me. Lydia and Charly approved." I grin at him.

"Good choice. Like the heels, too." His lips twist in a smile.

"So do I. It's amazing the things you can see from up here." I fake-punch him with my free hand.

He turns and pulls me to him. "You're also a lot easier to get to." He bends to kiss me, and I sigh as he touches my lips with his, first hesitantly, and then more firmly as I return his kisses.

I link my fingers around his neck and lean back to look at him. "You're easier to access, as well."

He leans in to kiss my forehead and rests his chin on top of my head. "Sometimes I think I'm losing my mind."

"Why's that?"

"Because I've always wondered what it would feel like to fall in love, and now I know."

I pull back to search his face, all trace of humor gone. Only tenderness remains. "Marc?"

"Chelsea, I've been in love one other time in my life." He shifted his eyes down and cleared his throat. "We were in college, and I thought I'd met the love of my life, we'd get married, settle into university life, have some kids, and live happily ever after. It was a plan, and it made sense."

"I'm thinking part of your plan fell apart?"

He nodded. "I found out my plans don't always work. When you're twenty-two, you think you have the world by the tail. God had other plans."

I snort. "You're preachin' to the choir, here. I thought Daniel was my last chance for love, marriage, and a family of my own. When it didn't work out, I swore off men."

His slow smile makes my stomach flutter. "Funny how two thirty-somethings can think they're so smart, isn't it?"

I pull my hands down to his chest, fingering his boutonniere, avoiding his eyes. "My parents were nineteen and twenty-two when they married, and have been married thirty-six years.

They'll tell you they didn't know anything when they got married, and yet, here they are. We try to figure everything out, and yet, here WE are, in our thirties, trying to second-guess God's plan, and fearful of every step."

"But perfect love casts out fear." He tilts my chin up to look into my eyes.

"First John 4:18." I study him. I've looked at his face before. This time, I really study. I find myself wanting to know what he thinks, what he loves, what he fears. "She hurt you badly, didn't she?"

"I'm embarrassed to say it, but yes, she did. I found out she was also seeing my best friend. They eloped during finals week our last semester. She wanted it over and done so her parents couldn't push her into marrying to please them."

"You were their pick, weren't you?"

He nodded. "Hometown boy, good family, a known quantity. They knew I was serious enough to keep her grounded." He gave me a half-smile. "In retrospect, their pushing me on her and her rebelling was the best thing that could have happened."

"How is being heartbroken a good thing?" While I'm more than happy he didn't marry this girl, whoever she was, the thought of him hurting caused me pain.

"Because it made me lean on God. He didn't hurt me, she did, but I had to learn to trust Him all over again. I was afraid to date for a long time, but I wasn't afraid of Him, because I knew He was trustworthy."

"I know. We both, literally, had to 'let go and let God,' didn't we?"

He nodded assent. "I love you, Chelsea. It may be too soon for you. You're getting over a relationship, and I completely understand if you aren't sure..."

I put my fingers on his mouth to stop his rattling on. "Marc, I love you, too." I laugh out loud as his eyebrows go up in surprise. "I didn't want to. You were that reclusive fuddy-duddy

English teacher and writer that wanted his own private island to write the next 'Great American Novel' and was going to sink my wedding business because you couldn't handle my noisy parties and receptions."

"Wow. That's a lot. I didn't want to love you, either. You're so much like my Granny Bert."

"Oh," I put my hand to my lips as tears spring to my eyes. "I can't think of a better compliment."

He hugs me close. "Granny Bert was generous, creative, and spontaneous. Her spontaneity always scared me a little."

"I understand. I'll try to engulf you slowly into my spontaneous creativity." I look up at him. "How's that?"

"I'll try to be patient with you when you have to have people around."

I have to laugh. "Bless you, Marc McCallum. I'll try to respect your need for alone-time."

"And I'll try to surprise you as often as possible."

"Ooo...I like that one."

Marc leans down to kiss me again when I feel a tap on my shoulder.

"Sorry to interrupt, but the bride and groom are asking for you two." Charly's arched eyebrow tells us we've not been as discreet as we thought.

My face is infused with heat. I'm glad it's getting darker.

"We'll be right there."

# CHAPTER NINETEEN

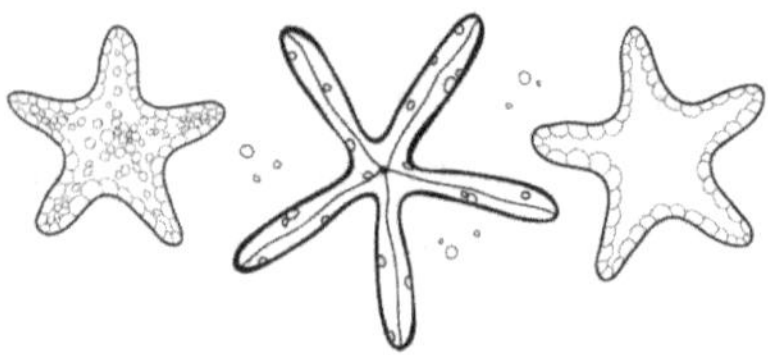

*One week later*

"**W**hy is it you love me again?" I shade my eyes against the glare of the sun as I watch Marc patiently painting the window trim I had glazed before falling off the ladder.

"Because you're smart enough to ask someone to help you do things you can't reach."

"Oh yeah." I can't keep the giggle inside. Watching him, muscular legs firmly standing on the proper rung of the ladder working on my dream project, I fall in love with him all over again.

I, who swore off men after inadvertently falling in love with a rat who did nothing but bring me down, am in love. For the last week I've pinched myself every time I encounter my one true love in Ms. Bertie's garden. I close my eyes for a minute. "God, thank you for your blessings. Forgive me for doubting You."

"Could you hand me that rag?"

I open my eyes to see him reaching down, and I pick the

scrap of cloth up and reach up to him in time to see the ladder waffle. "Marc, look out!"

Sandy soil and rocks and ladders sometimes do not mix. The ladder started tilting, and Marc's considerable bulk started pushing it off-kilter. "Look out below."

The ladder, Marc, the paint can, and me, all in a heap on the grass.

Marc rolls over close to where I am. "Are you okay?"

"I'm fine. You're the one that fell off the ladder this time, bucko." I scramble to my feet and laugh out loud when I see him. The right side of him was covered in white paint, which he doesn't notice until it begins to seep through his shorts and t-shirt.

He holds his arms out and looks down at himself. "Great. Did it get on the siding?" He starts inspecting the building.

"Nope, just on you -- and the grass." I put my finger to my chin in thought. "I guess I can put a table there for the next reception."

"For what purpose?"

"Well, mainly to cover up the paint on the grass. I'll think of something. Gifts, favors. There's always room for another small table." I look at him with a mischievous grin. "Those shorts and shirt, however, may be a lost cause unless you get them in the washer post-haste."

He pulls the shirt off immediately, carefully avoiding his hair and face. "Can we soak it in water? I've had this shirt for fifteen years. I got it when I went to Stonehenge, in England."

"You still wear a fifteen-year-old shirt?" I look at him, askance.

He seems surprised. "Don't you?"

"I don't think so." I stop to think. "Maybe to sleep in?" Then I look at him, truth dawning on me. "You ARE sentimental!"

He frowns. Twisting his lips to the side, he looks at me. "I guess I am." A slow smile crept onto his face and he continues looking at me, walking toward me threatening me with white paint. "Sentimental enough to write a historical romance after meeting you."

I begin backing up, forgetting there is a barberry bush behind me. When I reach it and touch the tiny needle-like prickles with my hand, I stop, trapped. "You wouldn't."

"Oh, but I would." He still has a comically lecherous gleam in his eye, and I'm beginning to soften, the closer he gets. "I'm sentimental enough to know you will never forget I proposed to you covered in white paint after falling off a ladder."

"Now you're being silly."

He leans in and kisses me, and while my lips are otherwise engaged, cutting off all thought process to the rest of me, he pulls me to himself until I feel the paint seeping through my clothes, as well. When my arms go up his bare shoulders and around his neck, he begins to chuckle, deep inside himself, and shifts his lips to the base of my neck. "Still think I'm silly?"

"If you'll keep doing that, I'll never call you silly again."

He lets me go, holding my hands in his. "Now, will you hand me the rag?"

I shake my head at him, handing him the rag. "Here you go."

He wipes the paint off his hands with the damp rag and reaches into the left pocket of his shorts. When he pulls out a tiny box and falls to one knee, my breath catches, and my eyes immediately seek his. "Marc?"

"Chelsea?" His eyes are dancing. He is being spontaneous, yet planned.

"It's too soon, isn't it?" I'm faltering, and I really don't know why. A tiny remnant of fear is there. I'm willing it to go away.

"I love you, Chelsea, and perfect love casts out fear, remember?" He narrows his eyes a little. "Marry me, Chelsea. Please?"

"What if..." I start to back-pedal, and he squeezes my hand.

"Chels, we don't know what tomorrow brings. What I do

know, right now, is that I love you, and I want to spend whatever time I have left on this earth with you."

I look down at our hands, linked between us, the tiny box lying on the ground, and I smile through a few tears. Looking down, half of him is covered in paint. The other half tanned from the sun of Pawleys Island beaches. Half of me wants to jump into his arms and never leave them. Ever. The other half? I kneel down in front of him and look up into his eyes. "I should have stayed standing, shouldn't I?"

He erupts in laughter, mine mingled with his.

"I love you, too, Marc. And yes." Tears were gathering in my eyes, and my throat simply closed up.

"Yes...?" He tilts his head.

"Yes, I'll marry you." It all comes out in a rush as I wrap my arms around his neck and hold him tightly. "I'll marry you, and I'll have your babies, and I'll take care of your yard. How's that?"

"I think I'm getting the best end of the deal." His lips crush mine.

When our kiss is finally spent, I add to my pledge. "I'll even live with you in Columbia while you teach."

"Good to know. Wouldn't want the kids to wonder why we're in separate cities." He puts his hand on either side of my face and kisses my lips tenderly. "This will be home, though. Our real home."

"Bless you." I get on my feet and stand in front of him. "Now, there was something you were going to present to me?"

"Oh yes. Actually two things."

I'm confused. "Two things?"

He pulls a piece of paper, actually an envelope containing a piece of paper, from his left pocket. "Glad it wasn't in my other pocket."

"No kidding. What is it?" My curiosity is getting the best of me.

He hands it to me, and I open it. It's a legal document, dated two weeks ago. I look down at him. This is dated before he ever kissed me the first time. I read it, silent, and then look down at him again.

"I know it doesn't really matter, now, but I wanted you to know I was prepared to give you lifetime use of the house and gardens for your business, in honor of Granny Bert."

"Marc, that's the sweetest thing..." I drop the paper on the ground and put both hands on his face and lift it for my kiss. "You believe in me."

"The way your eyes are shining now, I think I could have saved a bundle on the second thing." He winks at me when I whack his arm. He reaches down and picks up the small, gilded box, opening it with the spring, and takes a ring out of the box and places it on my finger.

"Oh, Marc." I look down at my finger, now adorned with the ring I have always dreamed of. A one-carat, round-cut diamond on a thin gold band. "It's my dream ring. How did you know?"

"I didn't." He stands and gathers me close, holding my ringed hand close between us. "It called out to me, and I knew it was the one."

"Better be careful. People are going to start thinking you're spontaneous or something."

"Or a man in love with a beautiful woman." He shrugs. "Either works for me."

# CHAPTER TWENTY

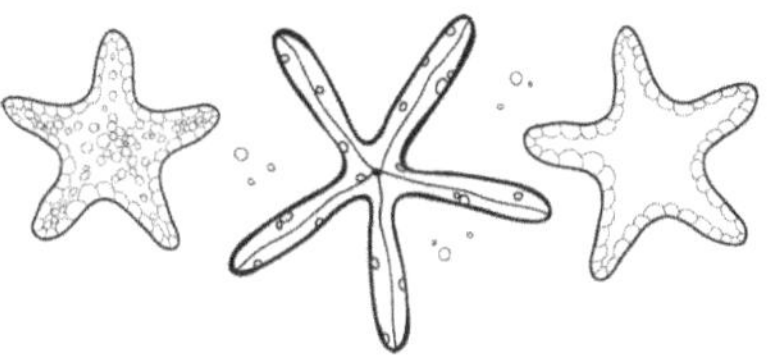

*Eight weeks later*

"Just think; after this, it won't be your apartment anymore, it will be the 'Bride's Room'." Lydia looks around what had been my cozy studio apartment with a sigh. Memories of her own wedding are still fresh.

Boxes are stacked in the corner, waiting to be taken next door. I had left what I would need for getting ready here, and the necessities will fit in a carry-on for the flight to Fiji. My bags are packed and sitting next to the door for our flight out of Charleston in the morning.

"Tell me again why we're going to Fiji when we have this perfect beach here?" I laugh as I primp my brunette bob finger-waves into place underneath my tiara holding my short veil. My tea-length vintage wedding dress is so...me. Shiny white, high-heeled, platform pumps complete the look, and when I look into the mirror at my mother, going through this twice in three month's time, I shake my head and smile.

"Because FIJI," that's why." Mom looks stunning, once again, but this time, with my vintage vibe inspired by some of

Ms. Bertie's pictures and dresses Marc and I found in the attic, we were all 1950's chic. Mom is dressed in a pink satin suit, Marc's mom in blue, both of which we found in trunks packed away carefully when they went out of style.

My nerves are beginning to surface, and each time I begin to get shaky, my matron of honor, Lydia, talks me down. "Since we're in Hurricane season here, it's probably a good thing you're gettin' outta Dodge. Fiji sounds amazing." She sighs, treating her lips to the bright red lipstick we'd chosen, checking herself in the mirror. Her purple floral full dress sports not one, but five petticoats, like mine.

"Hopefully none of you will have to worry about hurricanes while we're gone." I twirl a little, then chuckle. "I'll bet the guys aren't twirling in front of the mirror."

"They're not." Charly Butler, baby bump slightly visible, comes in to check on us. "I left your usher with them. I think there's a lot of pacing going on, and there's a ballgame on for the old married guys."

"Good. I've been nervous for the last eight weeks. It's about time Marc was a little rattled." I turn as Emma knocks and then enters.

"Everyone decent?" Her baby bump is a little further along than Charly's.

Sophie, Emma's teenage daughter, is right behind her mother. "I had to see you all before you go out. This is the coolest wedding ever!" She rushes over to me and hugs me. "You look gorgeous." Sophie has become my right-hand lately. At seventeen, she's working for her mom. Since we have many of the same clients, Emma loans her to me from time to time.

"Everything in place?" No one would let me go into the garden to see the reception space. He is living up to his promise to surprise me as often as possible. And to think I was going to find him a wife. Well, I guess I did, didn't I?

"It's perfect." Emma grins at me. "Marc is chomping at the bit."

"So am I. Can't we just start?"

"Soon." She looked at her watch. "I'm going to the back of the chapel, and Sophie will bring you all around when I give her the signal."

Lydia gave her a thumbs-up. "We're ready when you are."

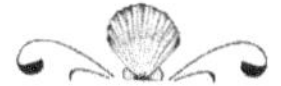

WHEN I SEE him at the head of the aisle, I feel my heart skip a beat. Beard trimmed, hair neat and tidy, Marc is resplendent in a white dinner coat and black tuxedo pants. The pink carnation makes me smile. When Sarah starts playing and singing "The Way You Look Tonight," I feel my knees begin to wobble, and Dad tightens his grip on to me.

"You okay, Hon?" He squeezes my hand on his arm.

I look at him through my short veil, tears swimming in my eyes. "Oh, Daddy, I'm more than okay."

He nods his head pertly. "Then let's get this party started. Ready?"

I nod back, afraid my voice will quiver and make us both cry.

It's late in the day, and we have candles. I think I'll always remember the way the candles look through my veil. It's comparable to looking through a star-lens in a camera. Soft, but with cross-hatches of light. It's beautiful. Will I remember any of my wedding ceremony, or will it be a conglomeration of sights, sounds, and feelings?

Maybe it will be a happy blur. I don't know, but what I do know is that when I look at Marc, now taking my hand and leading me onto the platform in front of our pastor, I realize I haven't felt any fear. Only excitement and an overwhelming desire to be married to this man, given to me by God.

Oh...There's a ring on my finger...Marc is lifting my

veil...Our lips touch in our first kiss as a married couple...The sound of applause.

No fear.

Just perfect love.

# Mr. Sandman

*A Novella*

## Regina Rudd Merrick

Scrivenings
PRESS
Quench your thirst for story.
www.ScriveningsPress.com

# CHAPTER ONE

Taylor Fordham stared at her computer screen, eyes glazed over as she scanned facts and figures. Those numbers equaled business for Pilot Oaks, the beautiful South Carolina antebellum mansion-turned-bed-and-breakfast and event center owned by the Crawford family.

Once again, she'd stayed up too late last night, watching her Sci-fi show, *StarPort: SP-1*, imagining how her favorite characters could end up together.

What was wrong with her? She loved her job. After Mike —*gotta get my mind off that*—she chose to stay in the Pawleys Island area, for Pilot Oaks. Nearby friends helped, but finding her niche in the hospitality industry and working for the Crawfords at their B&B made it worth staying.

"Excuse me ..."

Her head whipped up when a masculine voice filtered through her brain fog. Taylor looked around the bank of miniature decorative snowmen on her desk, her nod to holiday décor. The heat on her cheeks felt anything but professional.

*Way to go, Taylor.*

"I'm so sorry." She rose, smiling, her insides doing something weird when the brown-eyed, dark-haired young man smiled back.

*He's cute.*

"Not a problem." He gave her a half-smile. "I'm Ian Rutledge, here for the chef interview?"

*Okay, he's more than cute ...*

Her mind went blank for a second, then it all came back to her. She closed her eyes for a second to re-group. "Oh, I'm so sorry."

"There you go, apologizing again." He raised his eyebrow in amusement.

"I'm ..." She grimaced. "I'll let the Crawfords know you're here." She walked away before she could embarrass herself completely.

*It's the lack of sleep. I'm never this scattered.*

She followed her nose to the scent of gingerbread baking.

One thing you could say about the Crawfords, they believed in doing Christmas BIG. For some reason, Taylor could handle it with them. Robert and Linda Crawford, their daughter, Susan Harris, and the cook, Prudie Matthews, all looked up when Taylor entered the kitchen.

"Is he here?" Prudie asked.

"Mr. Rutledge is in the reception area. Shall I show him to your office or here?" It was a chef's position, after all. Wouldn't they want to quiz him about his specialty? Um, cooking?

Robert narrowed his eyes at the spry woman. "Now Prudie, are you sure you want to share your kitchen with a young whipper-snapper?"

The older woman laughed. "I think I can manage. The breakfast crowd is my favorite anyway. Large groups are getting to be too much for this old woman."

"You are not old." Linda shook her head, salt-and-pepper bob swinging. With one look, she put Prudie in her place. "You're less than twenty years older than me, and I plan to be a vibrant seventy-something when I get there."

"Sweetie." Prudie patted Linda's hand. "I'm old enough to be your mama and Susan's grandmamma, so don't argue. Besides, I might just have plans of my own." She twisted her lips in a smile and squeezed each woman's hand.

*Prudie? Blushing?* She had been such a comfort to Taylor, possibly because many years ago, she'd also lost the love of her life.

"Let's have him come back here." Robert sought approval from the ladies.

"Sounds good." Prudie smiled. "Bring him on back."

"Yes, ma'am."

Taylor retraced her steps, then detoured through the servant's back entrance to the study. She wondered what Mr. Rutledge would think when she appeared behind him, seemingly from the solid-oak paneling. She touched the hidden door, and the spring-loaded apparatus opening silently.

No need to worry about the man being shocked or surprised.

He was asleep.

# STARPORT: SP-1

Linc knew he shouldn't expect things to work out. When had they? But Alex was here, in his arms, where, he surmised, she belonged.

Now to figure out how to keep her there.

# CHAPTER TWO

*I*an floated on a raft along the Waccamaw River. No alligators or snakes to be found, not even a single mosquito. Everything was perfect, including the temperature and humidity. The overhanging trees draped with Spanish moss wafted overhead in the breeze, and nothing could drag him away.

*Except for that voice. That beautiful voice ...*

"Mr. Rutledge, are you all right?"

He opened his eyes from the dream only to stare into the concerned blue eyes of the young woman from before. She bent over, her hand gingerly touching his arm. Was it weird that after the eyes, her lips drew his concentration?

*I don't even know her name.*

"Sorry, I ..." He cleared his throat.

"There *you* go, apologizing." She put her hands on her hips and shook her head, laughter on her face. "By the way, I'm Taylor Fordham, the Event Manager."

He held his hand out as he stood. "Nice to meet you, Ms. Fordham." He'd already noticed the sparkling rock on her left hand. Married? Engaged?

*Of course, she is.*

His hand tingled as he held hers for a moment. A blush? Surprised, he let go, refusing to think about it any further.

"I think you know Prudie?"

"Yes." He grinned. "She's my grandfather's neighbor."

Ms. Fordham nodded. "She and the Crawfords would like you to join them in the kitchen. It's the slow time of day."

"Which way?" He pointed to the door.

"I'll take you back." She waved a hand, then led him into the main foyer. "Bad night?"

Small-talk. How do you tell people you might be working with that you hadn't slept since your last job ended on a sour note? Chalk it up to having one of the top ten most stressful jobs?

He shrugged. "Still not used to my bed at my grandfather's house."

"I understand." She seemed to have a difficult time meeting his eyes. "Here we are."

The door swung open to reveal a long worktable with Prudie, and he assumed the Crawfords. And another woman.

"Thank you, Ms.—"

"It's 'Miss.' You can call me Taylor."

*Engaged.*

"I'll leave you to it." She smiled.

"Thanks, Ms. … Taylor."

She raised her eyebrows. "You're welcome. And good luck." She left in a different direction from where they'd come.

Curiouser and curiouser. He reminded himself he wasn't here for a woman, especially one who wasn't available. Proving he deserved to be an executive chef was foremost on his mind. He turned to the table and smiled.

*Get it in gear, Rutledge.* His father's militant voice broke through the sleep-depravation fog, encouraging him to stand at attention. So he did.

"Mr. Crawford, ladies. I'm Ian Rutledge." Ian stepped

forward and held out his hand, which Mr. Crawford shook firmly.

"Nice to meet you, Ian." He introduced the ladies. "This is my wife, Linda, and my daughter, Susan Harris, the catering manager. And you know Prudie."

Ian smiled, relaxing a bit when Prudie spoke up. "I've known Ian since he was a little boy. His grandfather and I go way back." She glanced back at Ian. "Your grandma was one of my best friends."

"I remember." Back when his grandparents held annual Independence Day celebrations in their backyard, Prudie was always there, helping Grandma carry out platters of food. She was adept at swatting away little hands—mostly his—wanting to snitch a cookie before supper. He loved spending time there.

"Prudie tells us your last position was as executive chef at Montagu, in Charleston?" Susan asked the first question.

He gritted his teeth. That would have to be the first question. "Yes."

"I hated that it closed. My husband and I ate there a year ago. Excellent cuisine." Susan shook her head. "That's the restaurant business for you."

What else could he say? He nodded.

When Ian came back through the office, Taylor looked up from her desk. "How'd it go?"

"All right, I guess." He gave her a nervous smile. "We'll see." *Would it be unprofessional to loosen my tie?*

"I'm sure they'll let you know soon. Prudie wants to have a chef in place before the New Year's Eve Gala."

"I heard. Pretty big deal, huh?"

"Big for here." She chuckled. "Probably not for you, used to Charleston-big."

"Maybe." He glanced at the clock. "Again, thanks for your help."

She shrugged, eying him with concern. "No problem. Have a nice day."

He lifted a hand and made his way out the door.

When he got to his car in front of the antebellum mansion, he looked back at the tall columns on the porch and the comfortable rockers scattered along the front. The place was beautiful and inviting.

The Crawfords said Prudie would still take care of breakfast except for large groups. His position would allow Pilot Oaks to offer lunch and dinner options for overnight guests and private parties. He'd worked enough events to feel secure in his training. All he needed was confidence.

The sleepless year was another issue. What if he blanked out at a crucial time? It had never happened, but until lately, he'd never experienced long periods without sleep either.

Ian's unexpected unemployment came at a great time since Grandpa needed someone to stay with him after his hospitalization. He'd given up his Charleston apartment since his lease was up, and without work, he couldn't afford the rent. Besides that, the responsibility he felt for his perceived part in the failure of his friend's restaurant made him want to disappear. It wasn't a hard decision.

So, Ian moved to Murrells Inlet and searched for a job close enough to his family and far enough from Charleston. At first, he thought about trying a new career, but cooking was what he knew. A job at Pilot Oaks would put him smack dab in the middle of the food industry again.

Pulling the car onto Highway 17, he remembered errands, including groceries and Grandpa's pharmacy. He took a deep breath while heading north toward the commercial center of Pawleys Island.

His chest felt tight, so he loosened his tie. Just nerves, right?

The pounding headache wouldn't go away. Somehow, he'd passed Food Lion and Bi-Lo, both supermarkets closer to Grandpa's house, but he made it to Lowe's Foods, the last grocery establishment before crossing the rivers into Georgetown.

*Where's my brain?*

As he parked the car, he felt off.

*Deep breath, Rutledge.*

Nope. He couldn't do it. *What is going on?* He closed his eyes and tried to relax.

The vice on his chest would not stop tightening. His heart pounded. Why was he here? Food. No. Medicine. Oh, medicine AND food.

He glimpsed his reflection in the rearview mirror. Very pale. More than pale, he looked dead. A blinding, crushing feeling allowed only one conclusion. He was having a heart attack. Should he call 911? No. No health insurance. Could EMTs get here in time?

*While I can still think, I need to get to the hospital. Now.*

# STARPORT: SP-1

Dr. Elizabeth Garrity met the alien-but-all-too-human Bartok in the hallway, stopping him. "Bartok, are you okay? You look pale."

"That is a distinct impossibility, as my skin is darker than the night sky."

The doctor blushed and looked away for a moment, trying to gather her thoughts.

"Yes, but something is wrong ..."

## CHAPTER THREE

The breathing exercises Ian learned at the gym helped. He put the car in gear and headed south to the nearest hospital, Georgetown General. He hadn't been there since he sprained his ankle jumping into a shallow part of the river about twenty years ago.

*It's only ten miles to Georgetown from here. You can do this.*

Part of his brain argued the rationale of driving himself to the hospital, but the part of him in full-on survival mode took over. It wasn't so much that he couldn't see that worried him, but the dizziness. He made it over two bridges crossing the Great Pee Dee and the Waccamaw rivers, then he followed the signs to the hospital, and headed straight to the Emergency Room. When the car came to a stop, he put it in park and sat there.

*If I get out of the car, I'll pass out.*

A knock sounded on the car window. He tried to look up. Reality became more and more blurred with the dream from earlier. Wasn't he floating on the river?

*Wait. Someone is here. Pain. Can't breathe.*

"Sir, can you hear me?" A man in hospital scrubs tried to open the car door. "Unlock your door!"

What did the man want? Oh, unlock the door. That, he could do. Where was the button? Oh, he could just open the door.

As he pulled at the door latch, the man in scrubs caught him, or he would have fallen out of the car.

"GET ME A STRETCHER." The order shouted at close range sounded far away.

An oxygen mask slipped over his nose and mouth. Finally, he could breathe.

*In.*

*Out.*

"Sir, are you in pain?" A different nurse leaned over him, slid a cuff on his arm and grabbed his wrist.

He nodded.

"Where are you hurting?"

He put his hand on his chest and looked up at her.

"Get the doctor on call," she shouted. "Does it hurt anywhere else?"

"All over." He stared at her. Was he dying?

His attention drifted in and out as someone attached pads and wires to his chest and drew some blood.

The nurse fired more questions at him. He closed his eyes for a second. A lower voice joined hers. The doctor? When Ian opened his eyes, he met the concerned, yet familiar gaze of Rance Butler.

"Did you get demoted or something?" Ian's voice sounded raspy, even to him.

"Naw, I heard some Bozo having a potential heart attack drove himself to the Georgetown hospital from Pawleys." Dr. Butler arched a brow. "How are you feeling?"

"Not good." Ian tried to take a deep breath. Still couldn't. "You said potential. Am I having a heart attack?"

"Waiting for the blood work and EKG results." The doctor leaned on the rail close to Ian's head. He looked worried. "When did this start?"

"On my way home from a job interview." Ian looked up. The oxygen helped, but he still felt short of breath. "What's happening to me?"

"I'm not sure. I have an idea, but I'll let the test results advise me before I advise you. Sound like a plan?" Dr. Butler spoke the words, but Rance, the friend, put a hand on Ian's arm and squeezed.

The nurse arrived and handed a clipboard to the doctor, who thanked her.

*Am I dying? Tell me.* The words kept running through Ian's brain.

"I'll have the nurse give you something to relax you." Rance gestured to the woman beside him. "Jackie will give you the shot —I'm terrible at it. I'll be back in a bit." The doctor turned back to Ian. "You know, if you'd wanted to get together and talk about old times, we could have gone out for a milkshake."

"I'll remember that next time."

"If I have anything to do with it, there won't BE a next time." Giving his arm another squeeze, Dr. Butler nodded at the nurse.

"This will stick a little." The nurse spoke softly.

The shot was nothing compared to the crushing pain he'd been feeling. Before long, the pressure eased. Relaxation was bliss.

*In all the gin joints, in all the towns, in all the world, Rance Butler walks into mine.*

And he was out.

# STARPORT: SP-1

Dr. Elizabeth Garrity, Beth to her friends, placed her hand on Bartok's strong, sinewy appendage. "Are you sure about going through the drug trial? It's completely experimental."

"I am. If my people are to benefit from your research, then I must be willing to offer myself as a test subject." He stared into her eyes. "I am in good hands."

Blinking back tears, she nodded. When she picked up the needle to place the solution in the intravenous port, she paused and looked him in the eye. "If anything happens to you ..."

# CHAPTER FOUR

"No." Taylor shouted at the television screen, angry tears poised on her lashes. "Oh, no they didn't."

Every. Single. Time.

She sighed as the credits rolled, the clock reading 2 a.m. Taylor finished fifteen seasons of *StarPort: SP-1* for the umpteenth time, and, once again, was highly dissatisfied with the ending.

Only her closest friends knew of her obsession with the '90s sci-fi series. Why? Because … well … because she was a little embarrassed at the utter nerd within her.

She could organize everyone except herself, and all the know-how in the world was useless in the face of sleepless nights.

Too much.

Wide awake, Taylor channel surfed, pausing briefly on the Hallmark Channel. Ugh, Christmas movies. Small towns, snow, happy endings.

Where was *her* happy ending? Two Christmases ago, her happily-ever-after was just around the corner.

Until last summer when her life fell apart.

No sweet romance for her. She gave up on love, and put the SYFY channel in her list of favorites, removing Hallmark and Lifetime. Neither her life nor *StarPort: SP-1* went in the direction she wanted. Life you couldn't predict. Her show? She'd watched it in its entirety more times than she would admit, and still unreasonably and unashamedly hoped for a happy ending.

Taylor snagged her laptop from the coffee table laden with candy wrappers, a half-eaten bag of chips, and a glass of what used to be iced tea. The computer lay on a stack of magazines, safe from the former tea's condensation puddle. The only casualties were a few pieces of mail that she hoped weren't vital.

She scooched down on her comfy couch, a hand-me-down from her parents —and her favorite sofa ever—toes hooked on the edge of the coffee table. Maybe if she did a little Internet surfing, she'd get sleepy and get a few hours of sleep. But her brain couldn't stop running scenarios that would have given her the ending she wanted.

Why couldn't she get hooked on soap operas like people used to? They were on constantly during the day, and you didn't have to worry about endings. The shows just kept going. A baby born one year was four years old the next year, and the next year? Eighteen with a love interest.

She pulled up Google and stopped, her fingers resting idly on the computer. What to search for? She took a sip of her watered-down tea and tried to relax. Strumming her fingers, thinking, she gave in, typed *StarPort: SP-1*, and hit Enter.

Maybe there were more episodes that her streaming service didn't offer—as if she didn't know each episode inside and out. Cast interviews? Outtakes? Blooper reels? Maybe the creators had made a video or written a blog about what they had planned to happen, but didn't, because of the heartless studio execs.

Okay. In 1.5 seconds, nine million results came up from her *StarPort: SP-1* search. Nine. Million.

She scrolled down, yawning into the back of her hand as she

read past the Wiki page, the IMDB page, ads for buying the DVDs, and conspiracies as to why the show was canceled after a mere fifteen seasons. She delved into a rabbit hole.

After reading a few posts, she looked up, her lips tightening, and shook her head. These people didn't know what they were talking about. The characters of Linc, Alex, David, and Bartok should live forever. Who cares if the main actors were aging out of leading man and lady status?

Farther down the line, she paused.

Whoa.

There it was. On page two.

*Fanficwow.net.*

Stories. Hundreds of them.

About any television series you could think of. All by fans who felt the show had ended too soon. Just like her. The shows were listed in order of how many stories were published about that series. To her delight, *StarPort: SP-1* was third from the top, behind "Dr. What" and "Bunny the Werewolf Hunter."

She laughed, thinking how useless an actual bunny would be against a werewolf. That's Hollywood for you. Space and time, along with wormhole technology? Now *that* was reasonable.

She shook her head.

*I NEED SLEEP.*

Clicking on her choice, she saw over thirty thousand stories were devoted to *StarPort: SP-1.* Her heartbeat quickened in an excitement she hadn't felt since—and she hated to admit it— since Mike had proposed to her two years ago.

Out of the blue, he was gone. Taylor was devastated. Sure, she'd seemed to move on, but deep down? She was on a never-ending treadmill of home–work, work–home, weekday–week-end, Saturday–Sunday. The same thing, over and over again. The part-time job she'd taken monitoring sleep studies at the hospital —Thanks, Rance—bored her out of her mind, but it kept her from having so much time on her hands, alone.

She still wore the engagement ring. A few months ago, her mother asked when she planned to start dating again.

Date? It felt too much like cheating.

She had to get her mind off her personal drama. Maybe someone, somehow, had written a scenario in which Linc and Alexandra—Alex—finally got together after their fifteen-year slow-burn romance. That was enough drama for her, now.

# STARPORT: SP-1

Alex stood on her tiptoes to kiss McNeil and he pulled her to him to help her reach him more easily.

"When did you first know?" Alex ran her fingers through his short, military cut, loving the feel of his bristly, yet unbelievably soft, hair.

"When you told me off in the first staff meeting. I didn't want a woman on my team until I met you. Alex, you were the toughest woman I'd ever come across …

# CHAPTER FIVE

Taylor's stomach grumbled again. Thankfully, Pilot Oaks offered a soup-and-sandwich buffet, and today's special was potato soup. In addition to the gingerbread, she detected notes of oranges and cloves. Spiced cider?

Boycotting Christmas had crossed her mind several times this year, but the food? No way would she skip that.

"What did you think about Mr. Rutledge?" Susan caught up with her in the buffet line.

Taylor hesitated. "He seemed nice." Should she tell Susan about finding him asleep?

"I thought so too. His references are excellent."

Placing a half BLT on her plate, Taylor moved on to the steaming soup pot. "Shouldn't a chef cook something for an interview?"

Susan tilted her head. "I didn't think about that. Probably ..." She filled her plate. "Although, I ate at Montagu, where he cooked, and the food was excellent."

"I guess he couldn't be that bad, or he wouldn't have good references." Taylor picked up a glass of sweet tea. "Want to sit over there?"

Since Taylor began working for the Crawfords, she found herself gravitating to Susan. As the catering manager, they worked together a lot. The ten-year age gap didn't faze their relationship. Susan became the big sister Taylor never had. She played aunt to Susan's ten-year-old twin girls. Watching them and all the other kids in and out of Pilot Oaks made her long for her own.

At one time, she would have thought, *Someday.* But now?

*Now I just want to get from one day to another.*

"Like I told you yesterday before we released you, you had a panic attack."

"That's your diagnosis? You've got to be kidding me." Ian's heart thudded, and he resented its traitorous action. "Just shoot me. At least a heart attack is something you can't help."

"You can't help a panic attack, either." Rance narrowed his eyes. "Has this ever happened before?"

"No. I've never felt like that, and I hope I never do again." His mouth went dry thinking about it. "Can I expect this to happen every time I stress?"

Rance chuckled. "I don't think so. How have you been sleeping?"

Ian paused and took a deep breath. That felt good. "I haven't had a good night's sleep in six months."

Rance scribbled on a piece of paper.

*Somebody's going to have to translate that chicken-scratch.*

"I'm scheduling a sleep study." Rance looked at him more seriously than Ian had ever seen him. "I'm pretty sure your heart is fine, but this will help determine if the problem is physical—" Rance grinned. "—or mental."

"Believe me, it could go either way." Ian shook his head in

disgust, then considered his friend. "You've found your niche here, haven't you?"

"Yep. Sometimes I wonder why I've been blessed the way I have."

"And I wasn't even around to play wingman. You found Charly and the job on your own." Wasn't this the guy who was supposed to do big things? Shoot for the stars? Instead, he'd settled for a position in small-town Georgetown, South Carolina, and a home-town girl.

The smile that had won Rance more dates and gotten him out of more scrapes than Ian could count played across his lips. This was the guy who always landed on his feet. "I'm glad I was here, for you."

"Me too." Ian settled his gaze on Rance. "Is it necessary?"

"It is if you don't want this to happen again. It's either the sleep study or pills. Your choice. I'm assuming warm milk and counting sheep haven't helped?"

"I've tried every old-wives-tale remedy the Internet holds." Ian shook his head. *Face it, Rutledge, you're a wimp who can't sleep.* "What's involved with this study?"

"You come in around nine in the evening, and we hook you up to all kinds of monitors. No screens of any kind—computers, phone, television—during the test."

Once Ian agreed, he left Rance's office. The cold December air coming in the car window was invigorating, and it felt good to be alive. Ian knew he had insomnia but hadn't realized it could be serious.

As the sun lowered, Ian pulled into Huntington Beach State Park. He changed from his good shoes to the boat shoes he kept in the backseat. In a beach town, you never knew when you'd end up on the beach. He grabbed his jacket and climbed the dune to get to the beach, empty except for a few dog-walkers and a runner. Even better.

Walking to the edge of the cool Atlantic surf, he turned

toward Pawleys Island. Only the anti-social, the serious exercise nuts, or, like him, people in crisis mode, frequented this part of the beach. He stopped and stared into the horizon. He had the beach all to himself.

At least, he thought he did.

# STARPORT: SP-1

Alex walked around her kitchen island and sniffed this morning's bouquet from McNeil. So far, he'd sent flowers, candy, or ammunition weekly since they'd declared their love for one another.

Such a romantic ...

So why did she have this uneasy feeling?

# CHAPTER SIX

Taylor left her Litchfield Beach condo complex, Sandpiper Run, and walked toward Huntington Beach State Park. She was exhausted and had no energy. Not far beyond the beach house community lay a great stretch of coast too far for most beach-goers, making it a beacon of solitude for her.

The overcast sky was breaking up. Hopefully, before dark, she'd see blue sky. The brisk breeze heightened her senses. Her usual route took her north from her condo to Huntington Beach. That was the goal.

Taylor made it to the edge of the park property and stopped.

*Am I getting so soft that I can't walk without stopping?*

She stood there a minute, bent over with her hands on her knees. When she stood, she zipped her fleece jacket as an unwelcome chill went through her.

*Move or freeze.*

Straightening, she resolved to get at least halfway from where she stood to the public beach entrance.

*I can do this. I do this all the time.*

Legs heavy as lead, she slowed down as she reached her

goal. She'd kept her head down, watching. One. Step. At. A. Time.

"Hey."

Her head whipped up, and a smile tugged at her lips. Ian.

"What are you doing here?" She stopped, gasping for breath.

"Probably the same as you." He grinned, a pleasant sight. One little dimple, ever so slight, threatened to appear.

*I wonder if he has two dimples if he all-out smiles?*

She tried to catch her breath. "Hyperventilating?"

"No." Ian laughed. "But I've been standing here a few minutes."

Why couldn't she catch her breath? Her lungs and legs were conspiring against her. Talking was a chore. "I think I can make it back if I rest a minute." She stood next to him, staring out at the winter waves. "You found my favorite spot."

He looked down at her and nodded. "I found this place a long time ago."

"That's right, you have family here."

"My grandfather. As a kid, I spent summers at my grandparents' house. My cousins and I explored every nook and cranny out here on our bikes. It was a good way to spend the summer."

"Sounds like it." She looked up at him, smiling when his dark brown eyes met hers. "Where did you grow up?"

"Charleston. You?"

Unexpected, but not unheard-of. Not everybody in a big city knows everybody else. "Seriously? Me, too. What part?"

"Goose Creek. My dad taught at the Naval Nuclear Power Training Command." He looked at her and shrugged. "Before that, we were all over."

"Wow. I grew up in Mount Pleasant, the child of two high school English teachers." She snorted. "Nothing exciting there."

"But you didn't have to move every two years, did you?" When she shook her head, he twisted his lips. A smile? A grimace? Hard to tell. "What brought you to this area?"

"My fiancé lived and worked here. So I came, and I stayed."

*LIVED? Worked?* Ian wondered as Taylor referred to her engagement in the past tense. She must have a broken heart, yet hoped to reconcile with the guy. Wow. She didn't look like the total denial type, but you never knew.

"I have friends in Georgetown. If it weren't for that and my job with the Crawfords, I would have gone back to Charleston. Oh, and Rance." She unconsciously pushed a tendril of brown hair behind her ear, then took a deep breath and exhaled slowly.

"Rance?" Now he was really confused.

"Rance Butler. We've been close since grade school." She smiled sadly. "He's how I met Mike."

"Talk about a small world."

The slight crease between her brows intrigued him, and he wanted to see it go away. She intrigued him. They'd met in a professional setting, but out here? Here, they were just two souls trying to work things out.

*Wait. Who is Mike?*

"Rance and I met in college." He laughed. "I was his wingman."

She laughed out loud. "Do guys really DO that?"

With a straight face, he nodded. "Of course. A good wingman can mean the difference between a viable date and one you'd be better off avoiding."

"Seriously?"

"Seriously."

"And what are the perks of being the wingman?"

"Leftovers."

She laughed, and it did his heart good to see color in her cheeks.

Maybe she needed a distraction. "Rance has changed a lot in the last few years."

"In a lot of ways. Have you met his biological father?"

Ian nodded. "Some story, huh?"

"Can you imagine finding out the man you thought was your dad was actually your step-dad? Oh, and that you have a brother you've never met? Talk about messing a person up." She shook her head and stared out at the waves again. "How do you get past something like that?"

"Rance would say it's all about *grace*."

Taylor looked down at her feet, then back at the lowering sun. "I should head back. I just needed a rest."

"I don't mean to pry, but are you okay?"

"I'm fine. I haven't been sleeping well." She smiled and glanced over her shoulder again. "Better go. Hope to see you soon."

"Do you know something I don't know?" *Like if I got the job?*

She turned and walked backward a few steps in the sand, her smile relaxed. "No, but it's a small community."

He nodded, staring at her a minute, wanting to know her better.

Much better. But she was still hung up on Mike. The last thing Ian needed was a romance on the rebound. Better to keep her in the friend zone. No matter how much she intrigued him.

By the time Taylor returned, dark had overtaken her. She was, to put it mildly, exhausted. She stuck a small frozen pizza in the toaster oven and put a few dishes in the dishwasher. Then she went trolling through the apartment to see if there were any stray glasses or plates around. If she could at least do these dishes, she'd have one part of the apartment clean.

It was all she could do, these days, to get up and go to work. After work? She had nothing left.

Who needs clean dishes anyway? Pizza in hand, iced tea on a coaster, she opened her laptop. She'd check FanficWow and read more stories about *StarPort: SP-1*.

Some of the stuff was surprisingly good. *I've read books written like this.*

One particular writer, *SPfan89*, was a romantic. She tried to comment but was blocked. She would need to create a profile. Great. Another login and password to remember. She hesitated, and then gave in to the desire to comment. Who knows? Maybe this online community would fill a void she'd had since Mike died. How she missed him. He *got* her.

He'd loved her obsession with science fiction because it was so unexpected. It also made her very patient with his addiction to superheroes. He was a doctor but was fascinated with physics, so he loved the story of the Incredible Hulk. The quirk made her love him even more.

She picked *Lincsgirl* for her fangirl crush, General Lincoln McNeil. That would be a good username. Nope. Taken. She tapped her fingers against the keys. *Lincsgirl91*. What were the odds that it was available? She waited a few seconds and BAM. Accepted.

*Awesome!*

What to say ... She started typing, giving *SPfan89* all the reasons why his wonderful story wouldn't be realistic in real life, as much as she loved the story and wished it could happen.

She typed a few paragraphs and bulleted points, and then, before she could chicken out, bit her lip and clicked on *submit a comment*.

It was out there, in the ether, *awaiting moderation*, whatever that meant.

# STARPORT: SP-1

Dr. David Carter, an archaeologist, came around the corner, stopping short when he noticed his superior officers in a clinch. "Uh, guys."

Bartok, his alien strength always a surprise, put his heavy hand on David's shoulder. "Do not interrupt them."

"But they'll get in major trouble. I mean, if the General sees them..."

Bartok's brow arched almost menacingly. "Is not McNeil also a General?"

# CHAPTER SEVEN

Ian kicked up the footrest on the recliner after cleaning the kitchen. Grandpa snoozed in his bed after Prudie's supper of white bean soup and cornbread. After the day Ian had, he was more than happy to accept the gift of nourishment. He couldn't tell them about his episode yesterday. He'd need to work something out for tomorrow night so he could do the sleep study.

For now, Ian wanted to relax. Relax and not think.

He pulled out his laptop. After reading a couple of emails, he moseyed over to his favorite website. Maybe a newbie had posted a story on Fanficwow.net.

While Ian enjoyed binge-watching television and reading, he also liked to write. Nothing serious, just an online forum he'd found a few years ago where people posted stories, got feedback, and kept writing. He made a few cyber friends. They'd chat and email back and forth. It was much easier than facing his friends in real life with his failed career.

A notification. That was a surprise. He hadn't posted anything in a year, so he pulled it up, curious. When the long message came up, he almost laughed.

Here was someone—female from the looks of the username, *Lincsgirl91*—prepared to argue her case. While she would love to see Linc and Alex together, there were real-life obstacles they'd have to cross to make the relationship work.

*This is too good.*

TAYLOR WAS MISERABLE. This unfamiliar and all-consuming fatigue was getting to her. She'd almost fallen asleep at her desk. Almost.

"Good morning, Taylor."

"Morning, Susan." She smiled, trying to hide the fatigue. "Anything exciting happening today?"

"Just hiring a chef." Susan raised her eyebrows. "We're hiring Ian if he accepts the offer."

"Why wouldn't he?" What would it be like to see him every day? She admitted to herself, she was curious about that dimple.

"He'll be great. I'm going to call him, now." Susan paused waggling her eyebrows at her. "Want me to tell him you said 'hi!'?"

Taylor shook her head and gave her friend a disgusted look. "I think not. Thank you, anyway."

Susan plucked up a stuffed snowman from the collection on Taylor's desk. "Hey, you can't date a snowman, you know."

"If only." Taylor grinned. "One wrong move and into the greenhouse he goes."

"Ouch."

Taylor laughed at Susan, waving her off.

# STARPORT: SP-1

Dr. Carter, David, read through military rules and regs until he was cross-eyed. He'd always heard officers couldn't "fraternize," whatever that meant.

The last thing he wanted was for his comrades to miss the chance of a lifetime. Linc and Alex were together, a General and a Colonel, with or without the permission of the powers that be ...

# CHAPTER EIGHT

Ian arrived at the sleep clinic yawning. *Just watch. Tonight I'll sleep like a baby.*

If only.

Walking up, Ian smiled, seeing two familiar faces. Jackie, the nurse who had been in the ER with him the day before, and Taylor.

*Wait. Taylor?*

"You work here?"

"As needed. It gets me out of the house." Taylor shrugged. "Rance didn't mention you were the patient. He said to tell 'the patient' he'd be here as soon as Lamaze class is over." She leaned forward and spoke quietly. "I think tonight is when they watch 'the video'."

"What's 'the video'?"

"Childbirth." She chuckled. "Of course, since Rance is a doctor, it shouldn't bother him as much as it will Charly."

"Probably not. I understand they met when he was an intern here."

"He was on his OB/GYN rotation and delivered her brother's twins." She laughed. "Apparently her obstetrician was in his garden and got to the hospital just in time to see Rance catch twin number one."

"I got into the wrong profession." He grinned at her heightened color.

Picking up the clipboard, Taylor read the orders Rance left with her. "Jackie will hook you up to the monitors, so I suggest you get comfortable."

Ian looked down at his sweats and T-shirt and grinned. "I think this is about as comfortable as it gets." He held up his notebook and another book. "I brought entertainment without screens, per doctor's orders."

She held out her hand, and his first instinct was to take it, but he didn't ...

"Phone."

*Oh, yeah.*

He read a while, then wrote a while, and, settling in, Ian knew he should at least try to sleep. What if he'd forgotten how?

Pray.

That, he could do.

*God, let me sleep. Please. Whatever is keeping me awake, let me think about it tomorrow.* After praying, he started reciting several Bible verses he'd memorized. Starting with John 3:16, then random verses. He even hit the highlights of the Christmas story, finally landing on the twenty-third Psalm.

He makes me lie down in green pastures beside still water ...

If that wasn't peaceful, he didn't know what was.

TAYLOR SETTLED in with her laptop at the monitoring desk of the sleep lab, hoping to go over table arrangements for the Hurricane Rescue New Year's Eve Gala and catch up on reading her new favorite website.

The beeps and blips were above her pay-grade, but she knew

the basics. Heart rate was good. Blood pressure, good. He seemed pretty chill.

He'd pulled out a notebook and started scribbling in it. She noticed when his heart rate and BP went up, he had a look of intense concentration on his face. What was he writing? Maybe a letter to his girlfriend?

There. That would stop her from thinking about the good-looking chef.

Several times, she'd checked FanficWow, hoping for a message back from *SPfan89*, but alas, nothing. Maybe she'd made him angry and he'd never write again?

Taylor had done all she could with the Gala plans without input from Susan and was unable to settle on a new story to read. An idea popped into her mind. She began to type. Sure, she'd given *SPfan89* her reasons why Alec and Linc couldn't be together, but what was fanfiction for, anyway? She couldn't resist the chance to *right the wrongs* of the television writers.

Decision made, she highlighted her words, copied them to the forum, and hit submit.

She'd published the first chapter of her first story.

*Let's see what SPfan89 thinks of MY writing.*

# STARPORT: SP-1

"How is he?" Linc walked up to the doctor.

"His vitals are amazing, as usual." Dr. Garrity arched a brow.

"That's our Bartok." Shaking his head, Linc struggled with what he had to ask. "Will it work?"

"Only time will tell." She glanced up at him, a sheen of tears in her eyes. "The hardest part will be getting him to rest as he recovers ..."

# CHAPTER NINE

Taylor paid for letting Rance take Charly out after Lamaze class. With little to no sleep last night, exhaustion overtook her. It usually hit after lunch. This felt different, somehow. The spreadsheet on the screen in front of her blurred, and she wanted nothing more than to lay her head on her crossed arms and snooze. Instead, she closed her eyes and propped her head up with her hands.

*I'll just relax for a few minutes. That'll get me back on track.*

"Taylor?"

Her head jerked up. She checked the time on the computer screen. Ten minutes had passed.

*What have I done?*

"Taylor, are you okay?"

She looked up to see the concerned eyes, not of her employer, thank goodness, but Ian Rutledge. Her face heated and then cooled, nausea in her stomach growing. This was the most unprofessional thing she'd ever done.

"I can't believe I did that." She cringed.

"I feel your pain. Now we're even." His brows went down. "Is everything all right?"

*No, it isn't.* She couldn't say it.

When she stood, trying to cover her embarrassment, her knees buckled, sending her back down to her chair.

*Thank goodness I hadn't pushed it back.*

"Whoa." He was by her side in an instant. "Let me get you some water." He looked around at the exits.

"Through there."

"Right. Don't move."

Instead of the snarky remark that came to her lips, she nodded her head and watched as he rushed in the direction of the kitchen. He came back with a bottle of cold water, Prudie right behind him.

"What happened?" Prudie leaned in toward her.

"I fell asleep." *This is humiliating.*

"Are you sure that's all? Ian told me you were pale, and I have to agree." The older woman looked up at the hovering chef.

Tears smarted.

Linda chose that moment to come into the office. "What's wrong?"

"Taylor's not well." Prudie tilted her head at Taylor.

She opened her mouth to protest.

"Now don't you argue." Prudie's gaze cut to Linda. "Doesn't she look pale to you?"

Ever the mom, Linda touched the back of her hand to Taylor's forehead. "She's not feverish. If anything, you feel cold and clammy."

"I'll be fine."

"You need to take care of yourself and see the doctor. It's time you used that health insurance policy."

The boss had spoken.

Taylor glanced from Linda to Prudie, and then to Ian. They obviously agreed. At this point, she didn't have the energy to argue.

"Anemic?" Taylor knew the term meant her body was low in iron, but she hadn't been iron-deficient since ... ever.

Rance looked at the paper with the results of the blood work he'd ordered, then back at her. "Extremely, so we have a few choices." He was serious. His brilliant blue eyes had never been magical for her but were famous among all her female friends.

"And?" Her muscles tensed. Here it was the midst of the holidays, the fundraising gala coming up at work, and she still hadn't figured a way to get out of going home for Christmas.

"We can give you a blood transfusion ..."

"Yikes. No!"

"More common than you'd think. We can also do iron injections or iron tablets. Transfusion is fastest, injections a little slower, and pills the slowest, yet maybe the most reliable." He raised his eyebrows in question. "What'll it be?"

Quick decisions were not her forté. "How about we try the injections?" She didn't prefer shots, but if it would get her better faster, it might be worth it—without the horror of exchanging all her blood. Her skin crawled a little at the thought.

"Sounds good. Maybe we'll get you better in time to get home for Christmas." He chuckled, and then sobered when she looked away. "What's wrong?"

"Busy time at work. That's all." She wrinkled her nose. "And going home isn't the incentive you think it is."

He quirked a brow. "Is the Charleston crew still trying to fix you up with anybody and everybody?"

"You might say that." She cringed. Family holidays meant pitfalls and intrusive questions such as, 'Are you seeing anyone yet?' and 'Did you hear about so-and-so? They'll be grandparents next year.' "I suppose I'm being ungrateful."

"No, just human." He paused a moment. "Although, I know this guy ..."

"Don't even start with me." She struck him down with narrowed eyes.

"Just kidding." He winked at her. "You need to take some time off."

"But ..."

"No buts. I'd like to see you take at least a week off and do nothing but rest and maybe walk on the beach." Rance wasn't kidding this time. "I mean it, Taylor. If you don't take care of yourself, this can cause long-term health issues."

# STARPORT: SP-1

"I feel well." Bartok's frown remained. Was that a slight pout on his lips?

Beth wanted to laugh yet she smiled as his brows came down even further. "You're more than well, but I don't want you to be off-world and find yourself in a pickle."

"A ... pickle?" The pout turned to confusion.

# CHAPTER TEN

Grandpa's appointment with the orthopedic surgeon went well. He'd been upgraded to a walker or cane. No more wheelchairs.

"Now I can think about being Grand Marshall in the parade."

Ian's pulse picked up. "Are you sure?"

"Of course I am." Grandpa winked at him. "I've got plans, my boy. Big plans."

Big plans, huh? But he'd learned not to ask questions. When Grandpa was ready to share, he would.

Today had been a full day. He paused, thinking about Taylor's episode that morning, wincing as he remembered falling asleep in the office the day of his interview.

After the excitement of Taylor leaving, Susan Crawford offered him the job, which he accepted. The pay was good, the benefits amazing, and he'd be able to work alongside people he already liked and respected. How had Taylor fared after the incident this morning?

His sleep study had come back about the way he thought. Stress, burnout, etc. Rance had prescribed sleeping pills, low-dosage, for immediate relief, and a few sleeping tips. Basically, don't lay awake in bed. If you're not sleepy, get up and read until you are.

So, he tried that by catching up on his fanfiction. Was it contrary of him to try proving a point to *Lincsgirl91* by using all her reasons for Linc and Alex to NOT be together? He planned to make it as real-life as possible.

Logging in, he was surprised to see not only a message but the first part of a story—by *Lincsgirl91*.

The message:

*Hi. I'm sorry if I overstepped! Are you mad?*

He grinned. Yep, it was a girl, all right. Guys would ignore it and move on.

He rattled out an answer:

*Not mad, just busy last night. You make some good points. More later.*

Was it enough? Ian closed out the messaging window, then opened it back again. Strike while the iron is hot.

Ian, AKA *SPfan89*, began typing his rebuttal. He'd been thinking about it since her message yesterday and decided she deserved a thorough answer. Plus, if he overwhelmed her with words, maybe she'd keep her opinions to herself from now on.

StarPort: SP-1

Alex waited, hoping Linc wouldn't be late again. She knew the demands of command were great, and she sympathized. But as a woman? She longed to be more important to him. Chin in hand, she gazed out the window overlooking the San Francisco Bay and the Golden Gate Bridge. Beautiful.

His lips brushed her neck just below her ear, and she shivered.

He was right on time ...

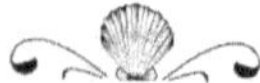

TAYLOR WALKED ON THE BEACH, read a novel, and took naps. At least she was sleeping.

Since she'd always wanted to try crochet, Prudie gave her a lesson.

It. Was. Horrendous.

What some considered a relaxing creative endeavor became, for Taylor, a stress-inducing pathway to irritation and increased blood pressure.

So, she stopped, reminding herself that needlework wasn't for everybody any more than Sci-Fi was.

She'd pulled up FanficWow to see if *SPfan89* had been around. His last message had made her laugh. Definitely male. Brief, to the point, no exclamation points. Her heart rate increased when she saw comments on her story. Already? She clicked on the icon, thrilled to see three comments, all positive, and two from other writers whose stories she'd read.

*How cool is this? They like me! They really like me!*

After the high of reading praise and encouragement from perfect strangers, she moved on to the messaging feature to see if the lengthy response could be from whom she hoped. It was.

As she read, she wondered if this guy was for real or not. Should she be angry? Reading more, she smiled. Finally, she began laughing and couldn't stop.

He ended his rant with this: *I planned to write a story using all of your reasons to keep them apart, but I couldn't. Maybe I'm an incurable optimist. Maybe I'm crazy, and maybe I'm trying too hard, but I intend to convince the world that it would be possible for Linc and Alex to be together. My next story will convince you.*

# STARPORT: SP-1

Linc gazed into her eyes. "I'll do anything ..."

"Don't say it, Linc." Alex's whispered voice pleaded with him. "We've been down this road before."

His hand caressed her cheek. "A road filled with potholes ..." His voice turned into a frustrated growl.

# CHAPTER ELEVEN

*I*an realized he was writing his story for an audience of one—namely *Lincsgirl91*. She left a comment on each post, and while she didn't always agree with him, she admitted when he made a good point. He returned the favor by one-upping the romance in his story for every twist she put in hers.

It had become a dance, of sorts. He couldn't help wondering about her. She'd mentioned a few personal things, but nothing concrete. Even so, he found himself looking for her in the message area as well as the story comments.

"Hey, Ian, mind if I join you?" Taylor broke into his thoughts.

He'd opted to eat in the kitchen rather than the dining room so he could catch up on his fanfiction reading. He gave his situation another minuscule thought but had no trouble pushing down the lid of the laptop and turning his attention to the hazel-eyed beauty in front of him, pouring herself a glass of water.

*Am I so easily swayed between two women?* Maybe *Lincsgirl91* wasn't hung up on another guy. But *Lincsgirl* wasn't here in the flesh, looking amazing.

"Hey. Are you back?"

"Ish." She wrinkled her nose adorably and shook her head. "Don't tell Rance, he wants me to take another week off." Shrugging, she sat down at the table with her bowl of soup. "Prudie makes the best potato soup."

"She is a wonder, isn't she?"

"She is." Taylor's mouth hung open. "I'm so sorry. I mean, you're a great cook too."

He held his hands up to ward off the apology. "There you go, apologizing again." He grinned broadly when her lighthearted laugh came forth. She was more relaxed than he'd ever seen her. Well, except for when she was asleep. That didn't count, did it?

"I'll try to stop." She pursed her lips and looked away for a moment. "Linda and Robert wanted me to take off until after Christmas, but I can't with the gala coming up soon after, so we compromised—part-time with breaks."

"It's a big deal, isn't it?"

"It is. Remember the hurricane that came through here six or seven years ago?"

He nodded as he blew on his soup. "I do. I came up here with a group to help flood victims clean out their houses. It was rough."

Taylor took a bite. "When I started working here, I learned Jared Benton ..."

"Isn't he the Crawford's son-in-law?"

"Yes, he's married to Sarah, Susan's younger sister. Anyway, he almost died in the storm."

Ian tried to imagine how it would feel to be so close to death. "Hurricanes are nothing to fool around with."

Taylor shook her head. "They're not. That year they lost their hurricane relief fund when it was embezzled by a police officer. Since then, the community has rallied around the sheriff and police stations to raise money so it never gets low again."

"Susan and I have been working on the menu for the event.

She says it will be the best one yet." Scooting his chair back, Ian stood and looked past Taylor at the clock. How had the time passed so quickly? "Speaking of the best one yet, some of us have to work for a living."

There it was again. Her laugh. It was infectious. No, not infectious. Habit-forming.

Taylor picked up her dishes and carried them to the sink. "Then I will leave you to it. Never let it be said I kept a chef from his appointed rounds." When she fluttered her fingers in a friendly wave, he had to smile.

"See you soon."

When her eyes met his, her smile grew slowly as she tilted her head. "Count on it."

WHO KNEW you could get a suntan in December? During her off time, Taylor walked up and down the beach daily. She'd also made a discovery that cut her to the core ... she liked sappy Christmas movies. Who knew?

Or maybe she was more comfortable thinking about romance these days.

On a particularly sunny day with weather in the upper sixties, she put up her Christmas tree. She covered it with seashells, starfish, and sand dollars, all found on the beach during her wanderings, then stepped back to survey her handiwork. It was progress. At one time she thought she'd never celebrate again.

Maybe there was something new on FanficWow.com. Her story was coming along nicely. She and *SPfan89* were corresponding regularly, and their stories were getting more and more convoluted and hilarious as the days went on. It was as if they were co-writing a story, and their *fans* were commenting to that effect. She shook her head. They had *fans*.

Taylor sat down and opened her laptop to find a message

from *SPfan89*. It stopped her in her tracks. He'd sent her an email address.

She pulled her hands from the keyboard and stared at the screen. Did she want to go up a level of intimacy and start emailing? He'd put the ball in her court.

The image of a certain dark-eyed chef with one dimple—maybe two—made her hesitate. She'd sworn off romance because it hurt too much when she lost Mike. What if God had other plans for her? Had he put two men in her path?

*To email or not to email.* That *is the question.*

TAYLOR WOKE up the next morning to a cold, cloudy day at the beach. More like December than the weather they'd been having. The wind blew, the surf roared, and it matched her mood.

Shivering in her fuzzy robe, she turned up the heat, then went to the coffee maker to brew her morning life-giving elixir. Sometimes the aroma of brewing coffee made her feel better. Today, it would take more than aromatherapy.

She put two pieces of bread in the toaster and pulled out her laptop. No email to speak of, unless she wanted to purchase an extended warranty on a piece of electronics she didn't own or borrow money at 25 percent interest.

As had become her habit, she clicked on FanficWow.net. She saw a post on *SPfan's* story and a numeral on the messenger notifications indicating a new message since last night. A delicious shiver went through her.

*Should I email him?*

She moved the laptop to the coffee table and looked down at the ring on her left hand. Mike was gone. He wasn't coming back, and he'd want her to be happy. *Wouldn't he?*

Working the ring off over her knuckle, she held it in front of her eyes, turning it this way and that, watching as the clouds parted and morning sunshine reflected shards of light and color all over her living room. She hadn't done that in a long time.

A new day was dawning, and the thought filled her with awe.

*Are you talking to me, God? Did you bring back the sunshine to let me know You're here?*

She put the ring back on. A sense of despair clung to her as if she were being punished for something she had no control over. It had increased the bitterness and sadness in her heart to the point that she extended only an outward appearance of faith. Here at Pawleys Island, away from family and life-long acquaintances, she could skip church when she simply didn't want to face people. Easier to keep to herself instead of getting out and meeting new people.

The beep from the coffee maker caught her attention. Toast cold and coffee brewed, she pushed the lever down for a quick re-heat and poured her coffee, popping the toaster and slathering apple butter on the overcooked bread.

*It's not burnt—it's perfect.*

Settling in on the sofa, she pulled the computer into her lap to read *SPfan's* message:

*Hey, Lincsgirl. Just checking on you. You mentioned not feeling well, and I hope you're better. I was being presumptuous and forward sending you that email address, and I apologize. Do you mind if I pray for you? See you on the forum.*

He apologized. Somehow his old-fashioned manners, and his asking permission to pray, cheered her. She felt a little energy flowing through her.

*Maybe it's time.*

# STARPORT: SP-1

Alex gazed up into McNeil's—no, Linc's—eyes.

Her feelings didn't change according to what she called this man. His hands rubbing up and down her back made her almost forget HER name, much less, his.

# CHAPTER TWELVE

A frown formed between Ian's brows. He'd worked all day with Susan, creating the menu and making lists of ingredients and serving pieces to order, and his brain was mush. Also, he'd shared an email address with *Lincsgirl*, but she still hadn't acknowledged it, either in a message or with an email. Maybe she was skittish about meeting someone online.

*Good grief. I created a new email address so I wouldn't be sharing my information with a stranger. And I'm questioning HER?*

"Will you be all right by yourself tonight?" Grandpa's voice interrupted his thoughts.

Ian chuckled. Who cared for whom? "I suppose so. Got a hot date or something?"

"Something."

Did Ian see a tinge of red on his elderly grandfather's face? He stared. Grandpa had a date. "Do you need me to drive you somewhere?"

He hesitated, looking at the clock on the wall. "No. I have a ride."

"Uh-huh." Ian tilted his head curiously. "Something going on I should know about?"

Grandpa gathered himself up and put on his fiercest patriarchal glare. "I think I'm old enough to have a few secrets from the younger generation."

"You'll get no argument from me." He lifted his hands up to ward off the ire emanating from his usually easy-going grandfather.

"Besides, isn't it about time you made your own friends around here and started dating yourself?"

The image of a certain event manager floated through his mind, and he squelched it, remembering the sparkling ring on her hand. The elusive *Lincsgirl* crossed his mind ...

"Working on it, Grandpa. It's been pretty busy at work."

"Excuses, excuses." Grandpa chuckled, belying his earlier statement. "Life's short, son. You're not getting any younger, you know."

Ian twisted his lips in a reluctant grin. "You're doing better than me."

Although Grandpa was hard-of-hearing, he perked up at the crunch of the driveway's shell-and-gravel mixture. "That's my ride."

"Need any help getting to the car?"

"No. I'll be fine." He held up a highly polished walking cane and headed to the door, a spring in his step despite his limp. He opened the door and waved, then turned. "I won't be too late."

"See that you're not. Curfews aren't for nothing, you know, young man."

The old man winked and gave him a thumbs-up. "Yes, sir." And he was out the door.

Ian strolled to the window to see his ride and saw a familiar red SUV in the driveway. Prudie.

*Grandpa and Prudie?*

"Go for it, Grandpa."

Back to the comfort of the recliner, he pulled out the laptop. He checked email—both his old address and his new one—and saw nothing of note. Disappointing. Still no movement on the new email address.

The last message mentioned taking time off from work, which explained why her story seemed to be updated quicker than his. He posted his in the middle of the night. *Lincsgirl*? She posted in the middle of the day.

A fleeting thought came to him. Was it possible? Could it be? No. That would be crazy.

*I'm crazy.*

TAYLOR FILLED out the online form and reviewed the information before she hit *submit* to create a new email address. She bit her lip, hesitating for a moment, but she hadn't revealed anything on there that would identify her if *SPfan* turned out to be a creep. There was always that possibility.

*I've watched Dateline. It's always the quiet ones ...*

A nervous giggle bubbled up from somewhere within as she clicked on the icon.

Working between the two tabs, she copied the email address *SPfan* sent into the *to* field. She took a deep breath. He'd given her an out if she didn't want to pursue a correspondence. But she did. As she thought about what to type, the light sparkled on the diamond in her engagement ring.

She held her hand in front of her, and a mist of tears impeded her vision.

*It's time.*

Taking her ring off, she stood and walked to her bedroom. She placed her engagement ring in the velvet slot in her jewelry case. Realization hit her. She wasn't engaged anymore. She simply owned an amazing ring given to her by someone she loved and would always love.

Tears flowed. Memories crashed in on her. Rance introducing her to Mike. Snow falling in Charleston on their first date anniversary. Mike kneeling in the cold, wet slush to propose to her, and then treating her to a white Christmas in the mountains with his family. Then the heartbreak of watching as the life drained from him on the street during the half-marathon that he'd been so excited to run.

She closed the case and pulled a tissue from the box, wiping her face. Staring at herself in the mirror, she nodded, agreeing with the voice within that another chapter in her life was about to start. But that didn't make it any less scary. What if she got hurt again? Was she strong enough to handle another heartbreak?

Maybe she should stick with making new friends. She'd keep Ian and *SPfan* in the friend-zone.

# CHAPTER THIRTEEN

*A*fter a busy morning of ordering food for the fundraiser, Ian was glad to sit alone in the kitchen with his sandwich.

He opened the laptop, surprised to see two new messages on his anonymous email account. The first "welcome to your new email account" message told him how to use email.

*I think I can handle it, but thank you for caring.*

But the second email? An unknown address flagged as potential spam. He smiled. *Lincsgirl91@hmail.com* was anything but.

*Hi,*

*I waffled back and forth over whether to email you or not. Please tell me you're not a creepy ax murderer?*

*LOL*

*It took me a little time to get my courage up. It's not in my nature to be so brave as to email a perfect stranger, but*

*it's not quite as scary as calling you on the phone, or,*
*perish the thought, meeting in person.*
*Sorry, but I wanted to put that out there. And as a friend*
*would say, "there you go apologizing again."*

*Let's see if we can't wrap up this crazy story before*
*Christmas, please? Ha!!*

*Lincsgirl.*

Ian was stunned.

Stunned, exhilarated, and a little nervous. 'There you go apologizing again' wasn't exactly a coined phrase, but it had become a joke between Taylor and himself since their first meeting. He'd been suspicious, but this? This was getting closer to proof, and if he were honest, a relief. And scary. There was still the engagement ring and the specter of Mike, who'd obviously bailed on her, but still held her heart.

Should he tell her? Get his secret out in the open? Would she freak out?

IN THE DOCTOR'S OFFICE, a little thrill shot up Taylor's spine as she read the email from *SPfan* a second and then a third time.

*Hi Lincsgirl,*

*Thanks for the email. I thought it might be easier to talk*
*this way instead of in the message part of the forum. I'm*
*never completely sure messaging there is private, not that*
*I plan to say anything untoward.*

*I agree. We need to finish up these stories. They're*

*starting to get a little over-the-top, aren't they? Although, I think the ten people reading and commenting will miss them when we're done. Maybe we should write one together? I know of other members of the forum who've done that.*

*Interesting that you wrote the Bartok and Dr. Garrity characters pairing. I always wondered why they didn't give the poor guy a girlfriend.*

*I have a lot going on at work, so if you email or message me and I don't get back to you, it's not you, it's me.*

*Are you feeling better? I was concerned when you said the dr wanted you to take some time off.*

*Gotta go. Lunch is so over.*

*SPfan*

If she were home, she'd answer him immediately. Would that seem needy? Let him wait a little while. Like until after her doctor's appointment.

"Ready to give me more blood?" The phlebotomist in the lab used the usual Dracula accent and always laughed at his own joke.

"Just don't take too much." She grinned at him. He was cute, in an endearing, fresh-out-of-school way.

"I'll be gentle." He drew more than one vial, then pulled out the needle and covered the wound with a cotton ball and tape. "I'll get the results to Dr. Butler before you make it to his office."

"Awesome." She pulled down her sleeve and reached for her jacket. "Thanks."

"Any time." He waved her away.

She walked out of the lab at Georgetown General and smack into Rance. "Whoa. What's the rush?"

He'd grabbed her upper arms to keep from knocking her over, a crazed look in his eyes. "It's time."

"Time for what? My appointment? I ..."

"No, Taylor. It's TIME." He looked over her shoulder to the exit. "I've got to go get Charly now."

"Go. I'll call your office and reschedule the appointment."

"Appointments. Office." He closed his eyes for a moment. "Forgot everything except water breaking and contractions starting and two bridges between her and me." He stared down at her. "Call my office and tell them what's going on. They know what to do."

She saluted. "Yes, sir."

He hugged her quickly and ran down the hallway to the exit. "You're a lifesaver."

"As long as I'm the tangerine-flavored one," she called out, knowing he hadn't heard a word.

# STARPORT: SP-1

Bartok's face was a rather fearsome sight, "Are you saying that I will be unable to fulfill my duties with the SP-1 team for two weeks?"

"I'm afraid so." Beth was sympathetic. She knew he'd placed his confidence in her, and that his identity came from his work with the team.

# CHAPTER FOURTEEN

"I'll be right there."

Ian hung up and hurried to Susan's office. "I got a call from Prudie that Grandpa has fallen. I need to meet them at the hospital."

"Oh, I hope he's okay!" Concern etched her face. "Go. And let me know how he is."

He paused and looked at the clock. Two in the afternoon, and they had guests. "About supper ..."

She dismissed his concern. "Don't even think about it. Mom and I have cooked for guests before. We only have two couples. Family comes first."

"Thanks so much."

"Go. We'll be praying for Mr. Rutledge." She patted his arm. "And for you."

He nodded and took off his chef's coat, made his way to the kitchen, and hung the coat on a hook next to the door.

*What have you done, now, Grandpa?*

TAYLOR PEEKED into the maternity waiting room to see Charly's sister-in-law Lucy pacing back and forth, her short blond bob bouncing with each step. "Hey."

"Hi, Taylor." Lucy's attention darted back and forth between her, the door leading to labor and delivery, and the entrance to the waiting room.

"Is everything okay?" Taylor took a cue from Lucy and clenched her hands together.

Lucy waved a hand. "Don't mind me." She shook her head. "They'll be fine. The doctor is here, and the rest of the family is on their way. Three weeks isn't dangerously early. The twins were three weeks early and look at them, now." She laughed.

"Speaking of the twins, where are they?"

"Sarah's got them."

"Ouch. Plus one of her own. That makes three two-year-olds."

"Yeah. Sarah always wanted a houseful of kids. I guess this is a good test." Lucy sighed in relief when her husband, Tom, came through the door with his mother, the beautiful Mrs. Mary Ann Livingston. "Finally. I thought you'd never get here. Is this payback for Charly being here alone waiting for the twins to arrive?" Lucy melted into her husband's side as he drew her close, laughing.

"What's the latest on my baby?" Mary Ann looked concerned. It was hard enough being a mama, but she was blind. "And by my baby, I mean Charlotte." She always called Charly by her given name, as was proper.

"Rance came out here a few minutes ago. The doctor is here, and things are moving pretty fast. So much for first babies taking a long time, huh?" Lucy crossed her arms in front of her, mild annoyance written all over her face.

"Good. Charlotte came pretty fast, but Tom, here? Took him a day and a half to decide to come."

"Well, he is a pretty big boy, after all." Lucy hugged her mother-in-law. "The twins were no walk in the park, either, but they're here, and they're healthy. That's the main thing."

"Amen."

Taylor's attention was drawn to the door when a nurse escorted another group into the room, Rance's family.

"Any word?" Without preamble, Rance's mother, Anna, wanted an update.

Taylor hugged her and smiled, since she'd known Ms. Anna most of her life. "Things are going well."

"That's a relief. I was so afraid the baby would be born before we got here." She looked up at her husband, Ashton Butler. "I hounded this poor man all the way here to drive faster."

"I told her I wanted to get here to celebrate a grandchild, not to be taken to the ER." His bright, welcoming smile dimmed slightly when Clifton Watson came through the door. Ashton walked over to Rance's biological father and shook his hand. "You made it."

"No way I'd miss my first grandchild's birth." Clifton looked ill-at-ease, but the last two years had done much toward healing the hurts from so many years ago.

"I'm glad you're here, Cliff." Anna's smile was genuine. Clifton nodded, relaxing.

"It's getting pretty crowded in here, so I'll head out." Taylor began to feel claustrophobic. She took Anna's hand. "Text me when the baby gets here?"

"I will, sweetheart. I can't believe they didn't want to know if it was a boy or girl. This being 'surprised' is for the birds if you have the opportunity."

Taylor laughed. "I'd want to know, too, but to each his—or her—own, right?"

She left the hospital, wondering how the day had filled up from sunup on.

When she reached her car in the hospital parking lot, she saw a car whip into a parking place close to the ER. Ian Rutledge exited the car and jogged to the door. She hoped everything was okay. With his grandfather's age and his health issues, it might be serious.

# CHAPTER FIFTEEN

Ian arrived at the emergency room at the same time as the ambulance carrying Grandpa. He rushed in, noting that Prudie exited the front of the ambulance along with the EMTs. Ian's stress level rose with each moment.

He reached the gurney carrying the patient sporting a large white bandage on his head, Prudie by his side. "Grandpa, what happened?"

Hiding a smile, Grandpa refused to meet his eyes. Instead, he winked at the lady next to him. "Just took a little tumble. Got too big for my britches, I guess."

"What were you doing?" Did he need to secure help for daytime as well as him being there at night? Was Grandpa's mind getting worse? With each question, his worry grew.

Grandpa's hand reached for Prudie's, and they looked at one another and laughed. "I'll be fine. I didn't break anything. I hit my head, and Prudie panicked."

"Your grandpa was trying to show me how to dance the two-step." She blushed.

"The two-step?" What could Ian say? *Young man, you knew better?* "Are you in any pain?"

"The leg took the brunt, and then my hard head."

"You didn't mess up where they did the surgery, did you?"

"I don't think so." Grandpa looked at him sternly. "Don't you go blaming Prudie. She told me to settle down."

"Oh, I don't blame Prudie." Ian cocked a brow at the gray-haired woman standing beside his grandpa. He wanted to laugh, now that he knew it wasn't serious.

"Good." Grandpa seemed satisfied as he looked up at the nurse who'd come to wheel him in. "Let's get this show on the road. I've got a parade to *grand marshal* in exactly five days."

"Now, Grandpa ..." Was riding in a parade on the doctor's list of approved activities?

"Don't you 'now Grandpa,' me, boy." He pointed his finger and wore the most impressive *Grandpa* look Ian had seen in a long time.

"We'll see what the doctor says."

The nurse glanced from one to the other. "Can I take you back now?" She raised her brows.

"Sorry." Ian stepped back and watched as they took him through the ER doors, then turned to Prudie. "The two-step? Really?"

She shook her head. "I know. I told him an old man with a cane had no business dancing at all, but he wanted to prove he could. Unfortunately, the coffee table got in the way of his fall."

"I'm glad he's not hurt any worse."

"Me too." She sighed, shaking her head. "Your Grandpa. He's a doodle, isn't he?" Her lips twisted in a grin as she patted Ian's shoulder. "He'll be fine. His head is as hard as they come."

THAT EVENING, after settling Grandpa into a room and doing a little shopping, Ian stepped off the elevator on the maternity floor carrying a bouquet in one hand, and in the other, a gift bag holding a baseball mitt. Rance's son might be a little young for it yet, but you couldn't start too early, in his opinion. To be honest, if the baby had been a girl, he'd have brought her a pink one.

Ian stopped at the nurse's station, where a pretty blonde glanced up and smiled. "May I help you?"

"Charly Butler?"

"Dr. Butler's wife." She grinned when he nodded. "She's in 304, down the hall and to your left." She bit her lip. "Do you need me to show you?"

"I think I can find it. Thank you."

"You're welcome. Let me know if there's anything I can do for you." Her brows lifted and he raised a hand and walked away. At one time he would have flirted right back at an attractive woman who showed interest in him. He was either getting old or getting more particular.

He knocked gently and heard Rance's quiet "come in."

Ian pushed open the door to see Charly asleep on the bed and Rance in the recliner holding a wad of blankets. He carefully placed the flowers and gift bag on the rolling tray next to the bed.

"I'm assuming there's a baby in there somewhere?" Ian eased over to his friend, who maneuvered the baby so he could show him off.

"Ian Rutledge, meet Reed Livingston Butler, my son." In a voice lower than a whisper, Rance spoke with emotion.

"He's awesome." Ian caught a hint of tears in his buddy's voice, and when he looked up, Rance was smiling and teary at the same time.

"He is, isn't he?" The new father held his son close, shaking his head. "Sometimes I have to pinch myself that I'm a husband and a father." He chuckled low. "Who knew?"

"Right?" Ian smiled. He wanted to mention knowing Taylor. How could he work it into the conversation? "I'm surprised the room isn't full of visitors."

"You just missed them. They were going out to celebrate, and come back later when they can, once again, fight over who gets to hold him longest." Rance chuckled. "Hey, how's the new job going?" He looked up quizzically. "Any more panic attacks?"

"Are you my buddy, or my doctor?"

"Both."

Ian grinned. "Great, and no, thank goodness." He spied a side chair by the door and tiptoed over to bring it nearer Rance.

"How's your grandfather?"

"You're off-duty, remember?"

"I know, but I'd ask even if I weren't a doctor."

"He's good. They're keeping him overnight for observation. Just a knock on the head." Ian couldn't help staring at his friend, the father. Weird.

"What about the job?"

"Love it."

Rance nodded. "I had a feeling. The Crawfords are good people."

"I'm finding that out." An opening. "I understand you know their event manager, Taylor Fordham?"

"Yeah!" Rance looked surprised. "We've been friends since middle school, I think."

"That's a long time." Ian eyed his friend. "Did you two ever date?"

Rance's laugh burst out before he could slap his hand over his mouth. Charly shifted in the bed, and the baby stiffened in surprise.

"Gotta remember to keep my laughs to myself." He watched as little Reed relaxed and went back to sleep.

"Hi, Ian. How long have you been here?" Charly pushed up to a sitting position. "Ooo! You brought presents!"

She sniffed the bouquet and handed it to Rance to place on the windowsill with a few other arrangements. When she opened the gift bag, she laughed. "What every newborn needs. A baseball glove."

"If he's a lefty, we'll have to get a different one."

"Thank you, Ian. You're very sweet."

"You're more than welcome. You've got a fine boy there, Charly."

"I think so too." She sighed, her attention divided between her guest and her husband comfortably holding the newborn.

"Sorry I woke you, babe." Rance winced.

She smiled. "I was starting to wake up anyway. I had to hear the answer to Ian's question about whether or not you and Taylor ever dated."

"Very funny." Rance turned his attention to Ian. "No, we never dated—except in emergencies. We were buddies, like you and me, only she refused to be my wingman."

"I can imagine. She seems nice."

The speculative gleam in Rance's eyes matched his arched brow. "She is nice." He stood and handed little Reed to his mother, who'd held out her arms as if she couldn't wait for another second to hold him again. Successful transition without waking the baby, they all relaxed. "Anything you want to know about Taylor?"

The unexpected question threw him off. He hadn't thought that far ahead. "Is she engaged?" Where did that question come from?

*You idiot, you've been wondering that ever since you saw her engagement ring.*

"Was." A sad expression crossed Rance's face. "Do you remember Mike Sloan? A couple of years ahead of us at Clemson?"

"Sure. I didn't know him as well as you."

"He was pre-med, like me, and kind of took me under his wing when he tutored me in Organic Chemistry."

Charly spoke up. "That sounds horrible."

"You have no idea, sweetheart. Anyway, I introduced them when we were at a pizza joint in Charleston one weekend." He drew in a breath. "Great guy."

"What happened?"

"He died."

# CHAPTER SIXTEEN

"*D*ied?" Dumbfounded. He'd been ready for a called off broken engagement and shattered heart, but not this. His soul ached for her. It was unfathomable that she'd suffered so much loss and pain at such a young age.

"It was during a half-marathon last summer. He had a massive heart attack right there on the street. Taylor was there. Heck, me and half of the hospital staff were there, and there was nothing we could do. Later, I found out he had an undiagnosed valve issue that chose that moment to blow."

"All the training he'd done, and his number comes up then." Rance closed his eyes for a moment. "He was a good guy. Good friend. Engaged to be married, great job as a hospitalist here at Georgetown General. The sky was the limit."

"I had no idea. I noticed her ring ..."

"Oh." A statement, not a question. Rance's eyebrows rose.

Heat started at the back of his neck and traveled upward. Hopefully, it would stop before it reached his face. "Guys notice these things."

"I've heard that." Charly laughed, then gave Rance a saucy

grin. "That's why when I caught this guy, I didn't let go for anything."

"I'm glad you got me." Rance leaned down and kissed her lips softly. "And I got you."

"Okay, single guy here." Ian waved his hand.

Rance cleared his throat and gave him a pointed look. "Taylor is great. She's funny and a little nerdy."

"How's that?"

"She was always trying to get me to watch this one show." Rance laughed, and realization dawned in his eyes. "That same show you used to watch on repeat all the time ... I can't remember the name of it ..."

Ian had to look away. "*StarPort: SP-1?*"

Rance pointed at him. "That's the one. Wonder if she still watches it?"

*Oh, she watches it, all right ...*

TAYLOR'S FEET moved forward as if walking through molasses. There was no spring in her step. Some of the feelings she thought she'd gotten past were rearing their ugly heads.

If Mike hadn't died ...

*Stop it. Stop it right now, Taylor Fordham. Sure, if Mike hadn't died, I'd be married and maybe even having my own baby by now. But he did, and I may as well accept it.*

One voice inside her head kept telling her to 'suck it up.'

Then there was another one. The one that let her wallow.

*I'll never find happiness again. I'll be old and alone with no children and no more love in my life. Why even try?*

That one had a name—no, several. Despair. Pain. Melancholy. Satan. Yeah, he tried to knock her off her feet every chance he got. She tried not to listen to him.

Exiting the elevator, she followed the signs and found Charly's hospital room without incident. She paused when she heard voices. *Good, nobody is asleep.*

She put on her public face and pushed the door open to see the new mom, baby, new dad, and a very discombobulated Ian. *Curious.*

"Hey, guys."

Charly held out the arm that wasn't holding Reed, and Taylor accepted the invitation for a hug. She needed hugs more often. Physical contact with a good friend lifted a little of the load off Taylor's heart.

"I had to come and see this little guy." She handed Charly the gift bag she carried and stole a peek at him. It was love at first sight. Tears filled her eyes, and she never knew she liked babies before. An only child, she had no nieces or nephews, but since she'd started working for the Crawfords, kids—toddlers to pre-teens—were all around her.

"What am I, chopped liver?" Rance put an arm around Taylor's shoulder, and she reached to hug him too.

"No, Rance." She looked down at the baby. "Y'all did good."

"We did, didn't we?" Charly beamed. "Do you want to hold him?"

Could she? "What if I drop him?" Her heart began beating a mile a minute, her desire to hold the baby escalating unex-pectedly.

"You won't drop him." Rance took the baby from his wife and held him out to Taylor.

Unable to resist, she took him in her arms, holding up his little head and relaxing into a natural sway that seemed to come out of nowhere.

Charly pulled the gift from the bag Taylor brought. "Baby Yoda!" She laughed and hugged the stuffed animal, her eyes going wide when it made the sounds of a newborn. "This is so cool."

"Only you." Rance chuckled.

"I'm determined to share my love of Sci-fi with the younger generation." Taylor smiled.

"If anybody can, it will be you." Rance watched her for a minute. "You're a natural."

"I agree." A lower voice joined the conversation.

She'd forgotten about Ian, and heat crawled up her neck and cheeks. He looked at her as if he'd never seen her before.

Drat those tear ducts. "I wouldn't go that far."

Ian walked over closer to her, looking at the baby, touching his tiny hand. Little Reed grasped his finger, and Ian looked at her in wonder. "Does this mean he likes me?"

"I'm sure it has nothing to do with the natural grasping reflex in all infants." Rance chuckled.

"Don't ruin the moment with medical jargon." Ian frowned. "I'll take what I can get."

Reed started wriggling and scrunched up his face, still not making a sound, but clearly waking, working hard at an activity Taylor wanted no part in at this juncture.

"I'm thinking he will need a parental figure—and soon."

"It's Rance's turn." Charly sent her husband a cheesy grin.

# CHAPTER SEVENTEEN

hen Charly's dinner tray arrived, Taylor took her leave. Ian following after her. The blonde at the nurses' station looked disappointed when he came down the hallway with Taylor.

He didn't know what to say. Taylor was *Lincsgirl91*.

*To tell her now, or wait?*

Wait. Definitely wait. She was still hung up on Mike. Even though the poor guy was dead. Despite his best—friendship only—intentions, Ian wanted more. But grief couldn't be rushed.

"How are the gala plans coming along?" Taylor broke the silence when they entered the elevator.

He stuffed his hands in his pockets and looked up at the ceiling of the moving cubical. "Good. We've got all the food ordered, and Susan is working on the layout."

Taylor covered her face with her hands, then looked up at him, her mouth in a thin line. "I'm supposed to be doing that."

"Hey." He touched her arm to get her attention. "It's not all on you."

"I know, but that's the fun part, and I'm missing out." She

gave him a sidelong glance and a half-smile. "How about that baby?"

"Way to change the subject." He laughed. They walked off the elevator and stopped.

"I'm a master at it." She grinned.

"Little Reed gets my vote."

She sighed, with a faraway look in her eyes. "Mine too."

If she could change the subject, so could he. "I'm going to check on Grandpa before I leave."

"Is he okay?"

Ian snorted. "He'll be good. They're keeping him for observation since he whacked his head on the coffee table."

"What in the world ...?"

"According to Prudie, he was teaching her the two-step." Their eyes met. Ian raised a brow, and Taylor laughed out loud. He had to join in. "I know. Crazy, huh?"

She quieted. "I hope to be that crazy when I'm his and Prudie's age."

"Me too." He hesitated, and it seemed that Taylor did, too. "Have you had supper yet?"

"No"

He didn't want to leave just yet. "Would you join me for dinner?"

"Why Mr. Rutledge. On such short acquaintance?" She used an exaggerated Southern accent and put her hand to her chest as if shocked at his suggestion.

"There's not a non-fraternization policy among Pilot Oaks employees, is there?" He narrowed his eyes, wondering if she'd take the bait. After all, that's what had kept their favorite characters apart for fifteen seasons.

"I don't think so." She tapped her chin with her finger, looking at him curiously. "I could be persuaded, as long as they serve sweet tea."

He smiled. "I think you're safe in this neighborhood." A

thought came to him. "Do you want to wait for me here, or tag along and meet Grandpa?"

She bit her lip, then met his gaze. "I'd love to meet your grandpa. Prudie talks about him all the time."

"Oh, she does, does she?" Ian held an elbow out and she took it. "You'll have to fill me in. I have a feeling there's some fraternization going on between those two ..."

"I'LL HAVE the crab cakes, please." Taylor handed her menu to the server and linked her fingers together, elbows on the table.

Ian perused the entree menu at Big Tuna, an eatery on the Harbor Walk in historic Georgetown. "Don't think less of me for not ordering seafood, but I think I'll have the ribeye." He looked the server in the eye. "Medium Rare." When the server nodded, Ian shook his head. "Write it down, because you can't uncook a steak, and I know your chef."

"Yes, sir." The young man grinned and wrote it down. "Can I get you an appetizer?"

"She-crab soup?" Ian looked across at Taylor, who smiled.

"That sounds good."

"She-crab Soup for both of us." Ian handed over his menu.

"And lots of sweet tea," Taylor interjected.

"Coming right up. Would you like me to send the chef out to see you?"

Ian laughed. "Let's wait until after the meal."

The server nodded, then hurried to the kitchen, leaving them alone.

Unsure what to talk about, Taylor looked around, then dove in. "This is nice. I haven't been here in a while."

"I like it. And I usually order seafood." Ian shrugged. "The chef is Greg Powers, a friend of mine. We went to culinary school together."

"Ah. It might be nice to eat with someone who has connections." Taylor grinned, more relaxed than she'd been in a long time. Though Ian didn't make her nervous, she kept fingering the spot where her ring had been. It felt so naked, it distracted her a little.

*Which is probably a good thing.*

The server brought the rich She-crab soup and bread, along with their drinks.

"This smells amazing." Taylor stirred her soup so it would cool. "So, your grandfather will be the grand marshal in the Murrells Inlet parade. How exciting for him."

A shadow crossed Ian's face. "Yeah ... I'm not sure it's a good idea, but he's determined."

"How did he hurt his leg?" Taylor blew on the spoonful of soup.

"He stepped off his fishing boat. A buoy shifted and knocked the boat crooked. Just one of those things when you're a fisherman. He was alone and lay there with a broken leg for three hours before anyone found him. Fortunately, he landed back in the boat instead of in the river."

"That's rough." There was something more in Ian's tone. She couldn't quite put her finger on it. "Does he usually have a partner?"

Ian shook his head. "No, but at his age, it would be better if he did." He dipped a piece of bread into the soup and took a bite. "Not much family left that's close by. I think we've all neglected him since Grandma passed away."

Taylor thought a minute. "He doesn't seem lonely." The garrulous old man won her over upon first meeting, and from what Prudie had said, he didn't have much chance to be alone, much less lonely.

"How could he not be?" Ian shrugged.

"How long has your grandmother been gone?"

"Three years. I thought about coming up here to work when I

got out of school, to be nearby for him, but then Greg and I had the opportunity to open the restaurant in Charleston."

"And now, here you are."

He scoffed. "Here I am." His half-smile came across as sad. "I'm here for Grandpa, but only because the restaurant folded, no thanks to me."

"I imagine there's more to it than that."

He quirked up one side of his mouth. "There is." He drew in a breath. "We started low on both experience and capital with expensive tastes in ingredients."

"It doesn't sound as though it was all on you."

Ian shrugged. "Maybe. I felt responsible, as the head chef. Greg's a good chef, but he tried to hold the business together while I kept ordering food. When I found out how much in the hole we were, it was too late to save it."

Tilting her head, she read sincerity and humility on his face. "Sounds like he should have kept you in the loop more."

"Maybe." He shook his head as if trying to throw off the serious topic. "Fortunately, he doesn't hold a grudge."

"I guess we'll find out when you get your steak." She smiled at him, hoping to lighten things up, and it worked.

For the first time since she met him, he laughed out loud, and her eyes widened.

*He DOES have a second dimple ...*

*Just friends. Just friends.*

Maybe if she kept repeating it to herself.

# CHAPTER EIGHTEEN

When Taylor didn't feel particularly sociable, she ate lunch in the kitchen's sunny breakfast nook. Prudie was gone for the day, and Ian was supervising the cleanup in the dining room.

Today, she needed time to think. She stood and gathered her plate and silverware, then stopped when a notification came up on her shiny—if a bit scratched—phone. An email. From *SPFan*. The time sent was last night, and she was just now getting it? Oh well. It wasn't the first time an important communique had gone rogue and appeared late. She felt a smile tug at her lips when she sat back down and opened the message.

*Dear Lincsgirl,*

*Hope you're feeling better. I'm sorry I've been out of pocket for a few days. Things are heating up at work, and by the time I get home, I'm falling asleep at the computer. Thank goodness we finished our stories. I concede to your superior storytelling skills. You not only gave Linc*

*and Alex a happily-ever-after but demolished each
reason they had stayed apart so long. I'm impressed.*

*I've been thinking, and before you start complimenting
me on using my brain, hear me out. I'd like us to meet. I
think we've shared enough about ourselves that we are
ready to connect. I can always use a new friend.*

*What do you think?
SPfan*

Taylor's lip would be raw if she didn't stop chewing on it.
*Meet?*

*SPfan* wanted to meet? It was scary and exciting at the same time.

*I'm not a thirteen-year-old girl meeting a predator.*

At least she hoped not.

Ian walked up to her, plate in hand. The cook always ate last.

"Hey, Ian."

"Hey." He had a nice smile. Dependable. Solid.

*Dimples.*

She couldn't help the chuckle that tumbled out.

"Are you okay?" He looked at her strangely but in a friendly way.

"I'm fine, thinking about something I read before you walked up." She took a sip of hot chocolate and gestured for him to join her across the table.

He settled in with his perfectly constructed sandwich, then looked across at her.

She had a fleeting thought. *Why do my sandwiches never look like that? Random.*

"Drinking your dessert today?"

Sighing with pleasure, she nodded. "I've got to get Prudie's hot chocolate recipe."

"Cinnamon and cayenne pepper."

"Come again?" Her mouth dropped open.

"Yep." He waited as she took another sip. "Notice the lingering heat after a few sips?"

"I'm going to experiment tonight." They'd become friends in the last weeks, solidified by their impromptu dinner a few nights ago. "May I ask your opinion on something?"

"Sure." He took a large bite of his turkey club.

Taylor hesitated. Was this too weird? *Too weird that I'm attracted to Ian and asking his opinion about meeting another guy that I may be attracted to as well?*

"… I met this guy online."

"Creeper?" He had an odd look on his face. Maybe it was her imagination.

"I don't think so?"

"You put a question mark on the end of your sentence. I heard it." Ian's expression gave nothing away.

"Anyway ..." She glared gently. "We've been emailing back and forth, and now he wants to meet." She scrunched up her face, hoping it wouldn't stick that way as her mother had always threatened.

He took another bit of sandwich and lowered his brows. "Do you want to meet this guy?" His deep brown eyes seemed to bore into her. At least he was showing interest now.

"Part of me wants to because we seem to have so much in common. Another part of me is anxious at the thought."

He nodded. "Sounds reasonable." Frowning, his gaze sank to the floor for a moment, then bounced back up at her. "What kind of things do you have in common?"

*Here we go.*

She had a hard time meeting his eyes. "We both like this ... television show."

IAN KNEW he'd made a mistake the moment he laughed out loud, so he got his act together quickly. The last thing he intended was to make fun. When he saw her reticence to admit her guilty pleasure, so much like his, it came out naturally—relief more than anything. He couldn't remember being this attracted to a woman. Her shy glow only intensified his feelings.

"You asked." Taylor set her cup down on the table and crossed her arms, leaning away from him.

"I'm sorry I laughed." He leaned forward. "So, you have this TV show in common."

"We met on a fanfiction forum."

"Fanfiction?"

She looked sheepish. "Fanfiction is where you take a TV show or book series, and write stories in that story world, with those characters. You can make them do anything you want."

"Like a little community of superfans?" He cocked an eyebrow.

"You make it sound like a bunch of forty-year-old guys living in their mom's basement playing video games."

"That wasn't the image I was getting." He grinned.

Laying her silverware on her plate, she gathered her things to leave the table. "Anyway, we exchanged emails and have had nice conversations. That's all."

He reached for her hand as she reached to pick up her mug and leave. "Taylor, if you think you want to meet this guy, do it."

Twisting her lips, her expression was unsure. "I don't know …"

"You only live once." He said nothing else until she looked up at him. "Who knows? He may be your soulmate?"

*From my mouth to God's ears …*

# STARPORT: SP-1

"Fly back to Denver with me?" Linc's boyish plea caused Alex to grin.

"Can't. I have a meeting with Major General Sherwood first thing in the morning. I thought while you were gone, I'd crash at your place if it's okay with you." She was able to sneak a quick kiss between sentences.

The military vehicle arrived all too soon to take McNeil to the airport.

"And here I was hoping to get you all to myself on a flight between here and Denver."

# CHAPTER NINETEEN

*J*t wasn't a glowing recommendation, but Ian's advice meant a lot to Taylor.

She put away the few groceries she'd bought, then checked both email accounts. On her personal one, her mom had emailed, asking for the fifth time what she wanted for Christmas.

*Running it pretty close, eh, Mom?*

And then the inevitable 'When are you coming home for Christmas?' and 'Will you be able to stay a week?' Like Mom thought she had school breaks.

She'd answer her mother later, after dinner. Now for the new, anonymous email. He hadn't emailed again, leaving his question hanging, and giving her plenty of time to consider it.

A tiny part of her wanted him to ask her again. Was that being selfish?

*Do it.*

Taylor hesitated, her fingers poised over the keys. Part of her wanted to close the laptop, forget this email address, and fade into the background. The other part? The other part wanted to move on. Wanted to see what would happen.

*Take a chance.*

Easier said than done. What if Ian was attracted to her, as she was to him? Shouldn't she allow him to ask her out, at least? After their dinner the other night, Taylor felt more comfortable with him, and he seemed to enjoy being with her as well. Was it wrong to be interested in two guys at the same time? How had she gotten past thinking of them as friends?

A long, desperate sigh whooshed its way out of her being. She made it much more difficult than necessary, and she knew it. Type already.

*Hi SPfan,*

*I'd love to meet the person who is as obsessed with this show as me. You tell me when and where, and I'll let you know how to recognize me ...*

TAYLOR'S EMAIL SURPRISED IAN. He knew how conflicted she was at the thought of meeting someone she'd only met online. He hovered the cursor over the unopened email, ready to click it open when he heard a voice.

"Ian, could you come back here for a minute?"

"Sure, Grandpa." He set his laptop on the table next to his chair and made his way there. "What do you need?"

"Your opinion." Grandpa looked a little discombobulated, which was unusual.

Ian laughed. "Since when do you need my opinion?"

"I can't decide what to wear to ride in the parade. I want to look good, not like an invalid riding in the back of a convertible, wrapped up in blankets." The older man narrowed his eyes. "Any ideas?"

"You're serious." Ian crossed his arms, suspicious. "What are you up to?"

"None of your business. I just want options."

"Options that won't make you look like an old man." He knew his eyebrows were lifted to his hairline by now.

Grandpa pinned him with a glance and nodded. "Bingo."

Most of grandpa's shirts were in the blue family. "It's supposed to be in the 50s on Saturday, so you'll need a jacket."

"I thought so too." Grandpa rifled through the articles of clothing. "Nothing is speaking to me."

A laugh threatened to explode from within Ian, but he kept it together. "How about your red sweater over this shirt, then your leather jacket?" He quirked a brow at him. "That youthful enough for you?" Ian's lips wobbled, trying to hide a grin. "If you want to look young, leave your shirttail untucked and don't wear socks."

"Let's not get carried away." Grandpa rolled his eyes. "I think wearing jeans instead of polyester is about as much of a concession as I can make in that department."

"Good call." Ian tilted his head. "Two-step, huh?"

Grandpa's eyes cut him a side-glance as he grinned. "Two-step."

Ian nodded, studying the old man's face, knowing that things were about to change. "You're sure you don't want me to drive you in the parade?"

"Nope. I want you out there watching, taking pictures for posterity."

"I can do that."

"And who knows, maybe that young lady I met will be at the parade too."

"Maybe."

"Nice girl." Grandpa arched one brow. "And I think you've noticed that."

Ian pushed his hands into his pockets and nodded his head. "Should I ask her if she knows the two-step?"

"Couldn't hurt." Grandpa winked and patted him on the

shoulder as he walked out of the bedroom, his limp barely visible.

TAYLOR READ his email again as she stood in front of her closet that evening, trying to select the perfect outfit.

*Hi Lincsgirl,*

*How about we meet at the Murrells Inlet Christmas parade? There's an ice cream shop on the Marshwalk, and it's never too cold for ice cream, is it?*

*Looking forward to seeing you ...*

Was she too easily swayed by a nice turn-of-phrase?

*Hi SPfan!*

*I can't wait! I'll be wearing a red hat and will be in front of Twister's. Is that the place you were talking about? How will I know you?*

In a matter of hours she'd meet *SPfan*. Her thoughts veered to Ian for a few minutes, making her wonder, but she'd already reasoned it out. She'd meet this guy and satisfy her curiosity with no expectations other than meeting a new friend with something cool in common.

She pulled out her favorite blue turtleneck sweater. The soft wool and deep color made her hazel eyes pop blue. At least that's what she'd been told. Blue sweater, jeans, and her favorite brown leather boots. Looking over the hats in her cold-weather-gear bin, she pulled out the second red hat she found. This one wasn't just red. It had snowflakes on it. She smiled. If she were to ask for a sign from God these days, it would include snow.

*That's silly. Isn't it, God?*

The hat she'd bought for the trip to the mountains with Mike. She fingered the soft knit. Before tears could form, she held it to her chest for a moment, thinking about the happy memories it brought to mind. She'd always love Mike. Always. And she knew recovery after losing someone so important to you is a process, and it doesn't have a timeframe.

She also knew that God loved her and wanted the best for her. Was she ready to learn what that *best* was?

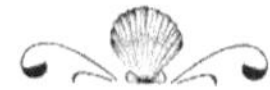

THE CALVARY CHURCH couples Christmas party was a good testing ground for the gala in a few weeks. He knew several of the attendees—Rance and Charly included—and Ian felt confident it would go well. The menu they'd settled on was one he could cook in his sleep—which he was doing on a more regular basis now. His mind was divided tonight. Part of him was keeping tabs on the kitchen, the other, thinking about meeting *Lincsgirl*, AKA Taylor on Saturday at the parade.

Soft Christmas music filtered into the kitchen every time the door swung open, and the extra staff they'd hired kept things running smoothly.

"Ian?"

A smile tugged at his lips when he heard Taylor's voice from the region of the door. Looking under the rack of pots between himself and where she stood, he crouched lower to see her face.

Sometimes just looking at her reduced his blood pressure. And sometimes, it increased it.

This time? The worried look on her face affected him all the way to the pit of his stomach.

"What's wrong?" Scanning the room, he was becoming more confused by the second. "Taylor?"

"There's smoke in the dining room."

Bile collected in his throat as he glanced at the wall holding four wall ovens and a bank of warming drawers. Looking around, he could see a haze up high, but the high-powered vent hoods near the ovens kept it clear in the kitchen. He rushed to the swinging kitchen doors leading to the dining room and his heart fell.

Sure enough, there was a thick haze of smoke hovering over the room. At that precise moment, the smoke alarms went off, alerting the diners who began looking around for exits and instructions.

Taylor took charge. She waved, then shouted to get their attention after the murmuring died down. "Folks, I don't think there's anything wrong, but we have an exit plan. Those of you on the last row of tables will exit through the French doors behind you, the next row to the door near the hostess station, and the ones nearest the kitchen to the hallway and out the front door."

Ian watched the evacuation like it was a dance in slow-motion. The hosts and hostesses had thought this through. Taylor was the emcee, and Robert, Jared Benton, and Mike Harris—Susan's husband—each took a door and made sure everyone exited in an orderly manner. He came to himself, realizing he had his own duties, but he couldn't get the girl with the micro-phone off his mind.

A crisis seemed to bring out the best in Taylor, which didn't surprise him. He evacuated the kitchen with the others, thankful they were dealing with smoke, which wouldn't set off the heat-triggered sprinkler system.

Once the kitchen and waitstaff were clear, he went through the stations working on various stages of meal prep. Cooktops, off, no evidence of scorching or burning. When he got to the ovens, however, his heart seized within him.

Smoke seeped out of one oven and then sucked out through the nearby ventilation system. He tried to pull open the oven door, but it was locked.

The Crawfords had two new ovens installed a week ago, not trusting the old ovens that had been in service for many years. It was top-of-the-line, but its day had come and gone, and now it was clear why new ovens were needed before the gala on New Year's.

At some point, when all the ovens were supposed to be turned off and the roasted pork loin left in a closed oven for another hour and a half, the door of this oven had inadvertently been locked and the self-cleaning feature activated. The temperature, instead of going down slowly from 450, had risen to well over 800 degrees.

He pulled at the door. Nothing. Tried the lock lever. Would not budge. There was still an hour left on the timer, and unless they wanted to ruin the oven, it would have to sit there and finish the cycle, incinerating one-fourth of the meat meant to serve the fifty people now shivering on the patio.

The pressure in his chest increased. In his head, he knew it was like the panic attack he'd had while driving a few weeks ago. In his current state of agitation, knowing what was riding on this one dinner, his head wasn't reliable.

The last thing he remembered was Taylor's hand on his shoulder, then nothing.

TAYLOR HAD SEEN a heart attack before. When Mike collapsed on the pavement, her world had turned upside down. He'd grasped at his chest, face sweating suddenly, and then, he was out. It had been so massive, she couldn't even get to him before he was dead.

Watching Ian grasp his chest and go down, it was *déjà vu*.

*No. I can't go through this again. I won't.*

"Help!"

Robert and Prudie came through the door. Robert to Ian's side, Prudie to the oven that was putting out more and more smoke. She pushed a few buttons, then turned to them. "Is he okay?"

"I called 911." Taylor's voice shook. She felt useless.

When Ian's eyes flickered, they met Taylor's, but she couldn't maintain his gaze. She turned, leaving the kitchen, but knew she would never forget the look of agony on her friend's face.

Was he more than a friend?

*No. I've gone through this once. Never again.*

She saw Susan in the hallway. "Taylor? Are you okay?"

"It's Ian … he's …" Tears came. "I have to leave."

Susan frowned. "Is he okay?"

"I don't know. He was unconscious." Raising teary eyes to her friend, she shook her head. "It was so much like Mike …"

IAN'S EYES closed again when he saw the look of abject fear on Taylor's face before she practically ran from the room. The pain had eased, but when the EMTs came in and checked his vitals, she was gone.

"What's going on?" Ian took in a deep breath when he heard Rance's voice.

"Taylor called 911. I think she thought I was having a heart attack." And it sure felt like it.

The EMT handed Rance his stethoscope. "I think you'll live

to cook another roast." He pulled Ian to a sitting position. "Another panic attack?"

Ian nodded. "This time it was definitely stress-induced." He looked around, seeing Rance, Prudie, Robert, and Linda looking at him with concern.

Susan rushed in and expelled the breath she seemed to be holding. "Thank the Lord." She stopped, hands on her hips, shaking her head. "I think you scared poor Taylor to death."

Was it possible to feel the blood drain from your face? "She thought I was having a heart attack." Ian closed his eyes and bowed his head, repeating his statement from earlier, then looked up at his friend

"I'll talk to her." Rance nodded.

"I sent her home." Susan spoke up. "She was close to falling apart and just said she had to go."

"One of these days when I think I'm having a panic attack, I may actually be having a heart attack." *Maybe Taylor should guard her heart against me, after all.*

"I think you're putting way too much importance on a couple of episodes." Rance reached his hand down to help Ian to his feet. "If you want me to run more tests, I'd be glad to."

"Ian, I wish you would. I don't want you to take any chances." Linda's mouth twisted in concern.

"Couldn't hurt." Rance looked more serious than he'd seen him in a while. "Better safe than sorry."

TAYLOR GOT BACK to her condo and couldn't stop shaking. Part of her wanted to go to the beach and walk off some of the horror that continued to fill her mind with images of Mike, then Ian, lying on a highway, dead.

The other part of her wanted to go to bed and pull the covers over her head for the foreseeable future.

She changed from her holiday hostess attire and pulled on a pair of well-worn jeans and a hooded sweatshirt with *Pawleys Island* emblazoned on the front.

The muted ding on her phone alerted her to a text message. Susan.

You okay?

Not sure.

There was a pause while Taylor watched the little dots dance, indicating someone was typing a message.

Ian's okay.

What happened?

He's having some tests run to make sure there's nothing wrong. He's up and about now.

I'm glad.

Looking around at the muted Christmas decorations in her living room, she felt angry. She'd almost given in to the holidays and to the idea of having someone in her life again.

"What's up with this, God? Am I being punished for something I did? If so, what IS it?"

She sat on her couch, head back, looking at the ceiling, hoping for some kind of divine guidance, or at least a little reassurance. What about the Holy Spirit, the Comforter? Where was He?

Nothing. Nothing but pain, heartache, and the pressing feeling of despair she'd almost forgotten. It wasn't as if she and Ian had a relationship beyond that of friendship. Not yet, anyway. She'd wondered … but no. *It would be better to be alone forever than to put myself through this hurt again.*

Life would go on. She wiped the tears from her eyes and took a breath. Her laptop called to her. Maybe she could get her mind off this latest sorrow.

Opening her email program, she felt her heart leap a little when she saw an email from *SPfan. Tomorrow's the big day. I finally get to meet SPfan.*

She didn't want to get her hopes up. After today, she'd be even more wary than before. Maybe she should be thankful for the friends she had and not put herself out there to hope for more. What was the point?

Settling into her favorite position on the sofa, she clicked on the unread email.

*Dear Lincsgirl,*

*Can I just say I'm more than a little excited that we get to meet day after tomorrow? I don't want to scare you off by being too anxious, but it's been a crazy week, and I'd like to think about something besides work.*

*I hope you're not disappointed.*

*Soon,*
*SPfan*

Taylor shut the laptop and leaned back, closing her eyes. She knew she wouldn't be disappointed. But what about him? Was he prepared to meet a shell-shocked woman who was afraid of new relationships because of the hurt she *might* experience?

Fingers hovering over the keyboard, she thought a minute before answering.

*Dear SPfan,*

*I'm looking forward to meeting you, too. It's been a strange day. We had a big event at work and a friend of mine collapsed. It was horrible. Oh, and then there was the smoke, but that's not the important thing. That sounded weird, didn't it? Let's just say there wasn't a fire. Like you, I hope you're not disappointed. Sometimes I wonder if it's worth it to have relationships if it's going to be so hard? Sorry. Way too serious.*

*See you at the parade. Or not. I'll be there, and if I've scared you off, I won't blame you!*

*Lincsgirl*

BLOOD DRAWN—AGAIN—AND stress test taken, Ian was exhausted by the time his lunch hour was over and he returned to Pilot Oaks. He'd refused to take off work because the kitchen needed a major cleaning after all the smoke from the night before.

"How was it?" Prudie's brows went up, and as usual, she spoke without preamble.

"Fine. Rance said he'd let me know how my tests were tomorrow.

"Good." She eyed him closely. "You sure you're okay today?"

He nodded. "Has anybody talked to Taylor?"

The serious look on Prudie's face almost crumbled when her lips quivered in a semi-smile. "Susan told her to take today off." She rinsed out the rag she held and placed it in the cleaning bucket. "She was feeling better."

"Good." Ian avoided the older woman's eyes. "I hated that I scared her like that."

Prudie patted him on the arm. "I know. She'll be okay."

"By the way, thanks for saving the evening." After Ian was forced to choose between going home and riding an ambulance to the hospital, Prudie had come through for him like nothing he could have asked for or expected.

"We cooks have to stick together. The meat wasn't all burned, so we managed to feed everyone after the smoke cleared."

"We?" Ian arched a brow at her. "I'm not sure anybody else could have pulled it off."

*Maybe I'm out of my league.*

"You stop that, ya hear?" Prudie glared at him. "That stove had been spoiling for a fight for a long time. It just chose that moment for the self-cleaning feature to work." She shook her head. "Lord knows it hasn't wanted to work for the last five years. Why would it choose last night to decide to lock up and prove it could do it?"

"Jealous of the new ovens?"

Prudie laughed out loud. "Exactly what I was thinking." She sobered. "Susan did say she wanted to see you when you came back after lunch."

Great. Time to look for another job?

# STARPORT: SP-1

Alex roamed the empty SanFranciso apartment as she made herself a cup of tea in the sparse kitchen—at least Linc had tea bags—and settled into the sofa, wishing he were there with her.

This apartment was more modern than his cabin outside Star-Port, but like the wilderness lodge, the apartment was relaxed, slightly messy, and, oddly enough, smelled faintly of wood smoke.

From where she had no idea.

# CHAPTER TWENTY

Ian delivered Grandpa to the parade lineup in plenty of time. His brows rose when he saw the Crawford's son-in-law, Jared Benton, and Prudie next to the Porsche convertible. Grandpa went straight to Prudie.

"So, you're the driver today?" Ian approached Jared, hand extended.

Jared chuckled. "Prudie said she wouldn't ride on the back of, as she put it, 'just any car with just anybody driving,' so I didn't have much choice."

"I hear you. Ian narrowed his eyes and cocked his head toward the older couple. "Is there something going on between those two?"

"I'm not saying." Jared shrugged. "My instructions were simply to drive and keep the heat going."

"Um-hmm. Keep an eye on them." Ian peered around at the crowd gathering, trying to keep his eyes open for a red hat. He hadn't answered *Lincsgirl's* question about how she'd know him, but he had an idea.

After her last email, he was a little concerned. She said she'd be there, but would she change her mind? He hadn't seen her since he'd been laid out on the floor of the kitchen the other night, and she had looked completely traumatized.

Ian turned to leave but with one last glance, he had to grin when he saw Prudie slathering sunscreen on Grandpa's bald head.

HEART FLUTTERING, Taylor arrived at the ice cream establishment and glanced around. *Anyone here look like a superfan of a defunct sci-fi television show?*

She'd tried all morning to tamp down her anxiety about meeting *SPfan* and shook off the worry that had taken over since Ian's attack.

There were at least one hundred red hats in the vicinity. It reminded her of the Union Station scene in Hitchcock's movie, *North by Northwest.*

Poor *SPfan*. She laughed out loud, surprising herself. He'd have a tough time picking her out of a crowd. She spotted Ian in the distance. Should he be here? Was he well? She could ask him, but she couldn't bring herself to approach him.

His grandfather was the grand marshal of the parade. *That's why he's here.* She lost him in the crowd. Her eyes roamed, hoping to see someone zeroing in on her. What were the odds, considering how many red-hatted persons were in the immediate vicinity?

The parade started. Local high school bands, scout troops, churches, and civic groups of all kinds had entered floats pulled by tractors and trucks. There were the requisite beauty queens in their tiaras and finery. Local politicians pitched candy to the children, who scrambled to pick it up before the next group came through.

Maybe *SPfan* wouldn't show up. Disappointment niggled at her, but she tried not to take it personally. It was a shot in the dark, after all. She'd probably scared him off with her last email.

190

# STARPORT: SP-1

When Alex flew back to Colorado after the morning meeting, Linc was at her house. She held him as close as humanly possible. Her meeting with General Sherwood proved to be life-changing. Linc had put his career on the line to be with her. The selfless act was more than she could fathom—although it had crossed her mind to do the same. He'd done it for her so they could be together without consequence.

# CHAPTER TWENTY-ONE

Ian was glad he knew the identity of his date because he couldn't believe how many red hats he saw in front of Twister's.

*Stands to reason. It is a Christmas parade, after all.*

He'd spotted her before finding a place to buy a rose, not wanting to arrive empty-handed. Keeping out of sight as much as possible, when he heard "White Christmas" playing, he knew he had to reveal himself.

Working his way through the crowd, he arrived behind her. She stood on her tip-toes trying to see the float from church and then sank back on her heels as she clapped. He watched her for a moment, taking in her natural beauty. There was a look of strain on her face, but then she smiled. When he heard a satisfied sigh come from her, he knew it was time. Fingering the ribbon on the de-thorned rose, he went for it.

Stepping closer, he slowly reached the hand holding the rose around her so she could see it.

TAYLOR SIGHED as the band transitioned from "White Christmas" to a drum-line rhythm. She was surprised when a red rose came from behind her, a masculine hand holding it.

Could it be? How did he pick her out from a veritable sea of red hats? All these thoughts tumbled through her head before she had a chance to turn and see who held the rose.

Wondering at the way things around her seemed to stop, Taylor held her breath. It seemed longer, but likely no more than five seconds before she turned around to see a familiar face.

*Was he ...? Could it be possible.*

"Ian?"

He offered the rose. "*Lincsgirl?*"

Taking the flower, her smile grew, and then dimmed. "You're *SPfan.*" It wasn't a question.

Ian nodded, and they stood there, staring at one another, both of them forgetting there were other people around.

What could she say? When Ian collapsed, she'd determined that no matter how she felt, she wouldn't put herself through the pain she'd experienced when Mike died. She couldn't do that again.

But Ian ...

When a car horn honked, their attention returned to the parade route.

THE ROSE BETWEEN THEM, Ian turned toward the street to see Jared's Porsche carrying Grandpa and Prudie. It halted, and both of them waved.

"What in the ..." He grabbed Taylor's hand and pulled her to the edge of the street.

"Somebody wants a picture taken." Jared shouted over the din and laughed as Prudie swatted at him.

"Grandpa?" Ian was still muddled. Between revealing

himself as *SPfan* to Taylor and his Grandpa's arm around a blushing Prudie, he didn't know what to think.

Grandpa hugged Prudie to him and kissed her before calling out to Ian. "Get our picture, Son. We need it for posterity."

After snapping a few pictures, Ian laughed when Grandpa held his lady-love's hand up to reveal a sparkling diamond ring. "That old sea-dog," he muttered under his breath, even as he laughed.

"Are they ..."

"I'd say they're engaged." Ian shook his head. "You know, Prudie said she'd never marry. I guess she didn't count on the Rutledge men."

"Pretty special, huh?" Taylor laughed as Ian turned toward her, smiling, and her hand somehow ending up in his. Her eyes narrowed. "Are you okay?"

"I'm sorry I scared you. It was a panic attack. I had one a few weeks ago brought on by insomnia. This one was stress-related." He brought her hand up to his lips. "You're not upset?"

She shook her head, her eyes bright with unshed tears. "No. Surprised? Yes. Relieved that you're okay? No question. But upset?" She paused, gazing into his eyes. "Absolutely not. I'm sorry I ran out on you. I was just so scared. But you're really okay?"

"No apology needed. Rance ran tests." He placed her hand against his heart. "My ticker is fine. I promise."

# STARPORT: SP-1

The sun was setting over the mountain holding the classified military installation they'd called their second home for nearly fifteen years. Across the valley, at Linc's cabin, Alex looked at her new husband and friends as they sat around a lake suspiciously absent of fish.

Bartok and Beth Garrity had discovered their feelings for one another, their shy happiness adorable.

Would they all get their happily-ever-after?

A shooting star assured her that, indeed, they already had.

## CHAPTER TWENTY-TWO

Taylor and Ian made their way to the end of the parade
route to see the happy couple, who still basked in the
congratulations they'd received.

"When is the big day?" Taylor admired the ring on Prudie's
hand.

Mr. Rutledge beamed down at his fiancée, and she nodded.
"New Year's Day."

"Are you serious?" Ian looked from one to the other and
laughed.

"We're not getting any younger, you know." His grandfather
winked at him, and Prudie swatted at him.

"Can I give the happy couple a ride home?" Jared gestured to
the car they'd emerged from minutes before.

Prudie nodded. "I think that would be nice, don't you, Ira?"

"You? Me? Back seat? I'm all yours, young lady." Mr.
Rutledge kissed her on the cheek and winked, laughing when she
blushed in front of everyone.

"Behave yourself, old man." Prudie shook her head but
couldn't wipe the smile off her face.

Jared helped them both into the car and waved at Taylor and

Ian, who stood there, watching as they drove off. The low rumble of the sports car belied the age of the passengers.

"If that don't beat all ..." Ian stared after them.

"I think it's sweet." Taylor looked up at Ian and narrowed her eyes. "So, how long have you known I was *Lincsgirl*?"

He twisted his lips in a smile. "Your first email to me."

"How ..."

"It was when you said, and I quote, 'there you go, apologizing again,' end quote." He lifted his eyebrows.

Her mouth dropped open in surprise, then she laughed. He looked down at his shoes, and then into her eyes. "I should have told you."

Tilting her head, she thought a moment. If he had, she wouldn't have had this time of anticipation. "No, I think it worked out perfectly."

His lips curved in a smile. "Walk on the beach?"

THEY WALKED in companionable silence for a little while when Taylor stopped. "Ian. Look."

She saw a snowflake on his shoulder, then another, and another. They looked around, mesmerized by the snowflakes falling all around them. It was a little private miracle especially for her.

"Are you okay?" Ian saw the tears she tried to hide.

"I'm fine." She smiled, trying to get the lump out of her throat. After being so worried about him, she was overwhelmed with both relief and anticipation. "Have you ever asked for a sign?"

His eyebrows went up. "You mean a sign from God?"

She nodded, hardly knowing where she was going with this. "When I see snow, I think of Noah and the rainbow." She shrugged. "A little nudge, telling me that God's here, and He loves me." She looked away, feeling her face warm. "Anyway, maybe I'll tell you about it sometime. It sounds a little crazy when I say it out loud."

"I don't think so." He turned her to face him, smiling as he brushed a fluffy flake from the tip of her nose.

When his brown eyes met hers, she couldn't look away. His smile faded into a look of wonder, which made her tremble with more than the cold wind off the Atlantic. She'd been so sure he wasn't the one. Couldn't be the one.

Ian took Taylor's hands and leaned in to kiss her gently. She smiled into his kiss, knowing, somehow, that she'd gotten her sign through the swirling snowflakes. Life would never be perfect on this side of Heaven. But at this moment? Pretty close.

When he stepped back, she pulled her hands free and rested them lightly on his chest, her heart in her throat. "I never did look into that non-fraternization policy, did you?" Taylor grinned as Ian laughed and pulled her closer.

"No, and I don't know if I can keep secret how I feel about you." His lips found hers once more. "I think I may love you, *Lincsgirl*."

Hugging him closely, she whispered in his ear. "Maybe you could call me 'Iansgirl,' instead ..."

# ABOUT THE AUTHOR

Regina Rudd Merrick began reading romance and thinking of book ideas as early as her teenage years when she attempted a happily-ever-after sequel to *Gone With the Wind*. That love of fiction parlayed into a career as a librarian, and ultimately as a full-time writer. She began attending local writing workshops and continued to hone her craft by writing several short and novel-length fan-fiction pieces published online, where she met other authors with a similar love for story, a Christian worldview, and happily-ever-after.

Married for forty years and active in their church, Regina and her husband have two grown daughters who share her love of music, writing, and the arts. They live in the small town of Marion, Kentucky, thirty minutes from the nearest Wal-Mart.

Connect with Regina through her website at hhttps://www.reginaruddmerrick.com, Facebook, Instagram, Goodreads, and Bookbub.

***Carolina Mercy***

**A Southern Breeze Series: Book Two**

She's always gotten everything she's wanted. He thinks he has to give up everything. Her best friend's wedding is foremost on Lucy Dixon's radar. Her biggest concern is once again meeting Tom Livingston, who has ignored her since an idyllic date on the boardwalk of Myrtle Beach the previous summer. At least, it is her biggest concern until tragedy strikes. Where is her loving, merciful God, now?

When Tom Livingston meets Lucy, the attraction is instant. Soon after, his mother is diagnosed with an untreatable illness, and his personal life is pushed aside. His work with the sheriff's department, his family– they are more important. He knows about the love of God, but circumstances make him feel as if God's mercy is for everyone else, not him. Can a wedding and a hurricane–blessing and tragedy–bring them together?

https://scrivenings.link/carolinamercy

*Carolina Grace*

**A Southern Breeze Series: Book Three**

First-year Special Education teacher Charly Livingston demonstrates God's love on the outside but is resentful that God allowed back-to-back tragedies in her family.

Rance Butler is a top-notch medical intern. He's on his way to the top, and when he meets Charly, he knows things will only get better. When he discovers family secrets and a dying father he never knew, his easy, carefree life seems to disintegrate.

Even in the idyllic ocean breezes and South Carolina sunshine, contentment turns to bitterness and confusion except for God's amazing grace.

https://scrivenings.link/carolinagrace

# RENOVATIONS SERIES:

**Heart Restoration**

*RenoVations Inc.—Book One*

For interior designer Lisa Reno things go from bad to worse when her contractor-brother falls off a ladder and breaks his leg. Now she has to deal with the past coming back to haunt her, an old house with a corpse in the creepy cellar, and her best friend trying her best to fix her up with any man that moves.

Nick Woodward is willing to do his old college roommate a favor—especially since it involves renovating his own inheritance. The last thing he wants is to get involved with anyone. When he lost his wife and unborn child so suddenly, he had made the decision to keep God and everyone else at arm's length. So far, so good.

Ah, the difference a trip to a dingy basement makes.

Get your copy here:

https://scrivenings.link/heartrestoration

**12 Days of Mandy Reno by Regina Rudd Merrick**

*RenoVations Inc.—Book Two*

Law student Amanda Reno is stuck in her tiny hometown in Kentucky to complete her studies virtually and work part-time at the Clementville Café. Her parents are stuck in Brazil, leaving Mandy to celebrate Christmas without them.

Young Sheriff Clay Lacey takes matters into his own hands, devising a plan to take Mandy's mind off her crushed expectations. She is no longer his classmate's tagalong kid sister, but a young woman he is increasingly attracted to.

How will Mandy react when she finds out Clay is the one working to make sure she has a memorable Christmas? Will she be pleased? Or will she cringe as she thanks the man who may be falling in love with her?

https://scrivenings.link/12daysofmandyreno

***Rebuilding Joy***

*RenoVations Inc.—Book Three*

**A waitress, a contractor, and an FBI agent walk into a café …**

Single mom Darcy Emerson Sloan has enough to do raising twins and running a restaurant. She's doing fine on her own and doesn't need the complications of a man in her life. But when her café turns into a crime scene, putting her and her children in danger, she begins to take interest in the handsome young FBI agent that comes on the scene.

Contractor Del Reno is as even-keeled as they come, but even he has his limits. And Darcy Sloan has pushed him too far. Every time he tries to help, it backfires. But now that Darcy and her kids are in trouble, he has no choice but to come to her aid and protect her. She's just going to have to deal with it.

Secret tunnels, organized crime, adorable children, and a wedding.

Just another day in Clementville.

**Coming in February 2024**

https://scrivenings.link/rebuildingjoy

# OTHER TITLES BY REGINA RUDD MERRICK:

### *Window of Peace*

*Stained-glass Legacy—Book Two*

Michael Connor "MC" Dunne led a charmed life. He had a plan—finish veterinary school, get married, and take over the local animal clinic. Enter the Vietnam War.

MC returns home, injured, to Park Haven, Tennessee, and soon learns there's a new vet in town, hired when the local veterinarian suffered a heart attack. So much for his plan.

Violent flashbacks and nightmares pull MC away from his faith and turn him into a hermit. His safe place is the family farm, working on the old cabin and restoring the chapel his great-uncle built in the early 1900s, with the family's heirloom stained-glass window.

Nancy Jean Baker struggles to prove herself as a competent

veterinarian to the small-town skeptics of Park Haven. Fighting her own demons from a traumatic past, she's driven to succeed.

But when war veteran MC Dunne returns home, wounded and wary, Nancy discovers she's standing between him and his dream.

Can they help each other overcome their hurts and horrors? Or is their hope of happiness doomed when the past threatens to ruin their future?

Get your copy here:

https://scrivenings.link/windowofpeace

***Novella Collections:***

***Love in Any Season***

**Includes "Spring has Sprung," a novella by**

**Regina Rudd Merrick**

https://scrivenings.link/loveinanyseason

**Candy Cane Wishes and Saltwater Dreams**

**Includes "Mr. Sandman," a novella by**

**Regina Rudd Merrick**

https://scrivenings.link/candycanewishes

***Coastal Promises***

**Includes "Pawley's Aisle," a novella by**

**Regina Rudd Merrick**

https://scrivenings.link/coastalpromises

*Stay up-to-date on your favorite books and authors with our free e-newsletters.*

ScriveningsPress.com

9 781649 173584